361

by Donald E. Westlake

A HARD CASE CRIME NOVEL

A HARD CASE CRIME BOOK
(HCC-009)
May 2005

Published by

Dorchester Publishing Co., Inc.
200 Madison Avenue
New York, NY 10016

in collaboration with Winterfall LLC

*This book is a work of fiction. Names, characters, places, and
incidents either are the products of the author's imagination or
are used fictitiously, and any resemblance to actual events or
persons, living or dead, is entirely coincidental.*

ISBN 0-8439-5357-8

Printed in the United States of America

Visit us on the web at www.HardCaseCrime.com

Raves For the Work of
DONALD E. WESTLAKE!

Somebody brought the car around from the hotel's garage. It was an Oldsmobile. Dad always bought Oldsmobiles. But I'd never seen this one before. It was last year's, black. When I'd been shipped to Germany, he had a two-tone blue.

The suitcases were loaded into the trunk, and Dad took care of the tipping. Then we got in, and pulled away, heading west crosstown on 53rd Street.

I started to roll the window down, and Dad said, "No, leave it up. Watch this."

I watched. He pressed a button on the dash, and I heard a whirring. Then a little chill breeze hit me in the forehead from a vent just above the door.

"Air conditioner," Dad said. "Three hundred dollars extra, and worth every penny of it. Changes the air in the car completely every minute."

"Lawyering does pretty good," I said.

"Chased a lot of ambulances lately," he said. He grinned at me, and slapped my knee. I grinned back. I felt good, to be in the states, to be with my father, to be a civilian Great.

We went up the Henry Hudson Parkway and over the George Washington Bridge. We took the lower level and Dad said, "This is new."

"This part of the bridge? It looks nutty."

We went up 9 to 17, and then west on 17 toward Binghamton.

Thirty-eight miles outside New York City, when we had the road to ourselves, a tan-and-cream Chrysler pulled up next to us, and the guy on our side stuck his hand out with a gun in it and started shooting.

Dad looked at me, and his eyes were huge and terrified. He opened his mouth and said, "Cap," in a high strange voice. Then blood gushed out of his mouth, like red vomit.

He fell staring in my lap, and the car swung off the road into a bridge support...

To Fred and Joanne and Nedra

.361 (Destruction of life; violent death.) Killing.

ROGET'S THESAURUS OF WORDS AND PHRASES

One

I got off the plane at Maguire, and sent a telegram to my dad from the terminal before they loaded us into buses. Two days later, the Air Force made me a civilian, and I walked toward the gate in my own clothes, a suitcase in each hand.

I was a mess. A twenty-three-year-old bum with mixed-up German and English in his head, two suitcases full of garbage, no plans. It felt fine.

I was at Manhattan Beach Air Force Station. That's in Brooklyn, southeast end, not far from Coney Island. Farther than hell from Manhattan.

I went through the gate and the snowtops didn't look twice, and then I wasn't in Manhattan Beach Air Force Station any more, I was on Oriental Avenue. Ahead to my left there was an asphalt oval by a field, where the buses turned around. There was a bus standing there, green. I went over and got aboard and asked the driver to let me off by a subway stop, I wanted to go to Manhattan. He said he would, and I sat in the sideways seat right behind him.

There were two airman thirds aboard, toward the back, and a Negro nurse, that's all. Then another guy with two suitcases came on, and he and I kind of avoided

11

looking at one another. I'd never seen him before, but he was another new civvy. We acted like we'd both just been circumcised, and if we talked to each other everybody would know.

It was a Tuesday afternoon, and July hot. It was only the twelfth, and my discharge date wasn't till the twenty-third, but the Air Force just gets you back the right month and lets it go at that. Outside, the blacktop was baking. You could see footprints, and in the distance there were rising shimmers. Car chrome gleamed for miles. The field between the bus and the Atlantic Ocean looked like dry brown hair.

After a while, the driver put his *News* away and started the bus. He swung the rest of the way around the oval, his arms moving as he turned the wheel, and his gray shirt was black with perspiration in circles below his shoulders. When he straightened the bus out and headed into the shimmer, a small breeze came in the open part of the window beside his elbow.

At one stop, he said, "There's your subway, over there," and pointed at steps going up to an el.

I thanked him, and toted the suitcases off. He called, "Good luck, soldier."

I smiled, but I didn't like him. I wasn't a soldier, I was an airman. On that route, by the base and all, he ought to know better.

The hell with it, I wasn't even an airman any more. I was a civilian now. I'd forgotten.

It was the Brighton Beach stop of the Brighton Beach Line. Coney Island was three stops to the left, end of the line. Manhattan was forever to the right. By the time I got the suitcases up the stairs, I was tired. I got two tokens, just in case, and went out on the platform.

There were some kids on the train, maybe fourteen years old, writing on the posters and screaming about it. I kept looking out the window, down at the neighborhoods. After a while it was all crummy residential—stone buildings, four and five stories, lots of windows, baby carriages and old kitchen chairs and Baby Ruth wrappers on the sidewalk. Then it went down into an open trench, and there wasn't anything to see. The kids got off at a stop called Newkirk. Then a little later it went underground all the way, and I read the ads above the windows. There was one I couldn't believe; a drawing of a hand with spread fingers, and surprinted over that in green block letters BELCH. Underneath, it said something was three times faster with stomach gas.

The train went over the Manhattan Bridge, with cars and trucks along a roadway right beside us. I felt like in a picture in a kid's geography book, and there'd be a DC-3 flying overhead and a tugboat underneath the bridge, and down at the bottom there'd be three lines of talk about transportation.

On the other side, it went underground again, and I took out the paper with the address Bill's wife had given me. I'd thought Bill was coming into town to get me, but when I called to check, his wife told me no, Bill was up at Plattsburg on a fleet sale deal with some trucking company, so Dad was coming down. She gave me the address of the hotel.

That was yesterday I'd called. It felt funny talking to her. My brother's wife. I'd never even met her. He'd met her himself six months after I got sent to Germany, and they got married eight months later. They were almost two years married now, and I'd never even met her.

Three years was a hell of a long time. I knew that now, in my bones.

Her name was Ann.

The paper said the hotel was at the corner of Lexington Avenue and East 52nd Street. The Weatherton. I got up and looked at the map down at the other end of the car. There was a Lexington Avenue Line, and it made a stop at 51st Street. That looked like the one.

I traced things out with my finger, figuring out where I was. I should change at Union Square for the Lexington Avenue Line.

It was the second stop after the bridge. I wandered around, looking at signs, carrying the suitcases, people bumping me. Then I saw a sign that pointed the way out, and I took it. The hell with it. Upstairs on the street, in the sun again, I waved at a cab and told him, "Lexington Avenue and East 52nd Street."

It was seventy-five cents on the meter. I gave him a dollar, and a bellhop took my suitcases in. There was a green awning out over the sidewalk, and a doorman in green and gold.

I told the guy at the desk that I'd come to join my father, Willard Kelly, Sr. Two bellboys and half a dollar later I was at the door of his room. "I'll knock," I told bellboy number two. "This is a reunion."

"Yes, sir." He pocketed the quarter and went away.

I knocked on the door, and Dad opened it. He grinned at me and said, "Ray. You son of a gun."

I grinned back till my cheeks hurt. I went into the room, with the suitcases on the ends of my arms, and he punched my shoulder and said, "You wrote you were gonna make Staff Sergeant. How come? You goofed up?"

I'd made Airman First with minimum time-in-grade all the way. There'd been time left on the enlistment for me to make Staff. Only I'd made it clear I wouldn't re-enlist. There's no sense wasting a rocker on a short timer. "I made civilian instead," I said.

"By God, Ray," he said, "you look great. You're taller, aren't you?"

"I don't think so. Wider, maybe."

"My God, yes. Look at the shoulders on the kid. Listen, wait till you see Betsy, five months old now." He grinned some more. "How's it feel, to be an uncle?"

"I don't know yet. I talked to Ann yesterday, on the phone. She sounded okay."

"She's a good girl. Bill's settled down, she's good for him." Then he shook his head and blinked, and came over to wrap his arms around me and pat the back of my head with his palm. "My God, boy," he said, and his voice broke.

I'd been trying to keep it in, but then I couldn't. We cried like a couple of women, and kept punching each other to prove we were men.

Then I wanted to go out for lunch and a beer, and Dad acted reluctant about it. He didn't want to leave the room. He looked okay, so I figured he was just tired from the driving, and the heat. The heat was bad, and the room was air-conditioned.

We ate at a place, and then Dad wanted to go right back to the hotel. I wanted to wander around a little and look at things, but it was three years, so I went back with him. But I kept looking around on the way back. I was born in New York, but Dad and Mom moved out when I wasn't even a year old yet. I didn't remember a thing about the city. Or much about Mom. She died when I was two.

In the afternoon, we sat around the room in our undershirts, with the air conditioner on. There were two wide beds, wider than singles but not as wide as doubles. I sprawled all over one of them, head propped up by a couple pillows. Dad wandered around the room, picking up ashtrays and glasses and phone books and then putting them down again. I didn't remember him so nervous.

Otherwise, he was the same. It didn't occur to me he should look different. It was as though three years hadn't happened at all. He was a guy, maybe fifty, with red-gray hair and a middle-aged paunch and plastic-framed glasses with old-fashioned round lenses. Same as always. I wore T-shirts, but he still wore the old kind, thin knit undershirts with just narrow shoulder straps, leaving the upper arms and shoulders bare. He had thick meaty shoulders, stooped a little, freckled.

We spent the afternoon filling me in. My big brother Bill was twenty-six now. He had a wife and a kid, and he was working for Carmine Truck Sales, and he got his driver's license back over a year ago. Uncle Henry was the same as ever. Like everybody, the same as ever.

When we went out for dinner, Dad wanted to go right back to the room again—talked about getting a good night's sleep for the drive tomorrow—but I said, "Look, it's only seven-thirty. Come on, Dad, this is my only chance to look at this place. We'll get back to the room by midnight, I promise."

So he shrugged and said okay, and we looked at Times Square and some other places, and I was disappointed. I'd expected something unique. Like Munich, that was unique. When I first got there, I looked at it, and I'd never seen anything that looked like that. But New York was just Binghamton bigger, like a little photograph put through an enlarger. It's all bigger, and you can see the grain and the bad spots better.

We got back to the hotel before midnight, and the next morning we checked out before nine. The breakfast eggs stayed with me, their taste, and made cigarettes taste awful.

Somebody brought the car around from the hotel's garage. It was an Oldsmobile. Dad always bought Oldsmobiles. But I'd never seen this one before. It was last year's, black. When I'd been shipped to Germany, he had a two-tone blue.

The suitcases were loaded into the trunk, and Dad took care of the tipping. Then we got in, and pulled away, heading west crosstown on 53rd Street.

I started to roll the window down, and Dad said, "No, leave it up. Watch this."

I watched. He pressed a button on the dash, and I heard a whirring. Then a little chill breeze hit me in the forehead from a vent just above the door.

"Air conditioner," Dad said. "Three hundred dollars extra, and worth every penny of it. Changes the air in the car completely every minute."

"Lawyering does pretty good," I said.

"Chased a lot of ambulances lately," he said. He grinned at me, and slapped my knee. I grinned back. I felt good, to be in the states, to be with my father, to be a civilian. Great.

We went up the Henry Hudson Parkway and over the George Washington Bridge. We took the lower level and Dad said, "This is new."

"This part of the bridge? It looks nutty."

We went up 9 to 17, and then west on 17 toward Binghamton.

Thirty-eight miles outside New York City, when we had the road to ourselves, a tan-and-cream Chrysler pulled up next to us, and the guy on our side stuck his hand out with a gun in it and started shooting.

Dad looked at me, and his eyes were huge and terrified. He opened his mouth and said, "Cap," in a high strange voice. Then blood gushed out of his mouth, like red vomit.

He fell staring in my lap, and the car swung off the road into a bridge support.

Two

I remember being moved. The doctor said that was impossible, it was a false memory, but I remember it. And a guy saying, "Look at the leg."

Then there was a long gray time, and then a time when I knew I was in a hospital bed, but I didn't care. Nurse rustlings, glass clinkings, paper cracklings, they all happened far away in some other world. The same with movement, white against white, people passing the foot of the bed.

Then I realized I wasn't seeing with my right eye. All the layers of fuzzy white were in a plane, I didn't have any depth perspective. When I closed just the left eye, it went away.

I made a sound, and it was awful. Then there was hurried rustling, and a balloon of flesh hung over me, with smudgy eyes. A woman's voice asked, "Are we awake?"

I didn't say anything. I was afraid to make that sound again. I blinked my left eye. I told my right eye to blink, but the message got lost someplace. I couldn't feel anything around there at all.

The balloon went away. When it came back with a doctor, I was in better shape. Every time I blinked, the left eye worked better. I could make out the wall, and the iron tubing of the foot of the bed, and the high right angle of the door frame. The balloon came in, being a nurse, and then the doctor.

I was just reaching my hand up, slowly, to find out what was wrong with my right eye. The doctor shoved it down under the sheet again. "Now, now," he said. "None of that. Let's not overwork."

"Eye," I said. Then I thought he might misunderstand, might think I was talking about me, so I said, "See." I was going through the alphabet.

"We'll get to that," he said. "How do you feel?"

"See," I said.

"We don't know yet. Are you in pain?"

I was. I hadn't noticed till then, and all of a sudden I

noticed. My legs hurt, like fury. Down by the ankles, and spreading up to above the knees. And the right side of my head, a dull ache like ocean waves.

"We'll give you something," he said.

I guess he did. I went back to sleep.

Every time I woke up, it was a little better. I woke up, went to sleep, five or six times, and then one time Bill came in. They wouldn't let me sit up yet, and I felt like a little kid again, lying flat in the bed, my big brother standing there grinning at me. "They make us tough, Ray," he said.

I said, "Dad?"

He stopped grinning, shook his head. "Shot," he said.

But I knew it already. I could still see him, falling sideways toward me, his eyes painted pieces of plaster. He was dead then, before the car even left the road.

"How long've I been here?"

"A month. Five weeks tomorrow."

"This is August?"

"Tuesday, the sixteenth." His grin was a little weaker this time. "You had a rough time, boy. They didn't know if you'd live."

"Listen," I said. "They won't tell me. My eye, the right eye. It's all bandaged."

He went away, diagonally across the room to a chair with a green back. He brought it over, sat in it beside the bed. Our heads were on the same level. I was getting used to figuring out perspective with only the left eye. Two, three days before, he would have just gotten smaller, and then bigger again. Now, I could think of him going away and coming back.

Three years had changed him. His red hair was bushier, his face paler and the freckles fading, his cheeks jowlier. He looked tougher and more sober. He looked more reliable.

He said, "They said I could tell you if you asked, but not otherwise. And only if I thought you could take it."

"It's gone?"

He nodded. "You went through the windshield. A piece of glass."

"Good Jesus." I lay there and thought about it. I was missing an eye, forever. Never again that eye, never again.

I'd always have to fake perspective.

It might have been both of them. Hell, it might have been the life. I was still around, I could still see.

What the hell did I look like these days?

I asked him. He said, "Like a turkey's ass, plucked. But better every day. The doctor says you won't have any scars that show. And I've already talked to a guy about a glass eye. He'll fit you for it the minute the doctor says okay."

"Jesus.... The feet? They hurt like hell." I knew they were still there. One time, I'd got my right hand up behind my head—that was before I could move the left hand too well—and pushed my head up so I could look down my length, and the feet were still there. I'd been worried about amputation. I'd heard of people whose legs hurt after they'd been cut off and they didn't have any legs any more. Mine hurt, and I couldn't move them, so I was worried they were gone. But they were there, fat tubular bulges under the sheet, encased in bandaging.

"Your ankles were broken," Bill said. "Crushed between the car and the bridge support. They've been doing bone grafts on you."

"And I'll be okay?"

"Sure." He grinned one-sided at me. "You'll live to play the piano again," he told me. "With your feet, like always."

Then I asked him for a cigarette and he said no. So I got one from the cop who came in that evening. His name was Kirk, and he was State Police, CID, in civvies. He had me tell the story, and there wasn't that much to tell. I hadn't recognized either of the men in the Chrysler. I didn't know what "Cap" meant. I didn't know why two strangers would shoot my father.

When he left, Miss Benson, the thin one, grabbed the cigarette out of my mouth.

Bill came by every day, for about a week. Then one day he didn't come around. I asked Miss Benson. She said, "He had to go back to Binghamton."

"Why?"

She got evasive, and I kept asking her. So she told me, and wouldn't look me in the eye. "I'm sorry, Mr. Kelly. His wife was hit by a car. She was killed."

"Oh," I said. "I never met her."

Three

When I got out of the hospital, three days after Labor Day, I had two eyes, one of them working. With that one,

I saw the guy get out of the Plymouth across the street from the hospital and come walking toward me. I slowed down, feeling naked. I still remembered the one who stuck his hand out the side window with a gun in it.

This one was different. Medium height, thin. He'd lost weight recently, and hadn't been able to afford a new wardrobe. His jacket hung on him like a style that had never caught on. His hair was sandy; his scalp was probably sand. His face was sharp of nose and chin and eye and bone, but there was weak pulp behind it, peeking through.

He stopped in front of me, looking at the tie Miss Benson had picked out. She'd had to buy me some clothes. My two suitcases got burned in the car. I'd given her the money, some that Bill had sent me.

He acted as though he wanted to talk to me, but was afraid somebody might notice. I said, "Okay," and sidestepped him and walked across the street to the Plymouth. I might have been afraid of him, but he was afraid of me. He came trotting after me, on shorter legs. I could hear him breathing.

I went around the Plymouth and got in the right side. He slid in behind the wheel, next to me. He looked very worried. He got out a pack of Philip Morris Commanders. On him, they were wishful thinking. He pawed one out with two fingers and thumb, and I took the pack away and got one for myself. We lit up in a leaden silence, with him trying to watch the whole outside world at once, and then, jerkily, he said, "I owe your old man a favor. I come to do it."

"What sort of favor?"

23

"A long time back. It don't make no difference now. You're his son. I just want to tell you, you ought to go away. Change your name, clear out for good. Go someplace out west, maybe. But don't go to New York."

"Why not?"

He lipped his cigarette, made it look terrible. His eyes jerked around in their sockets like ball bearings. At last, he said, "There's gonna be trouble. You don't want to get mixed in."

"What kind of trouble?"

"That's the favor," he said quickly. "Even-Stephen. If they saw me talkin' to you, they'd gun me. I've done enough, maybe too much."

"If *who* saw you? The men who killed my father?"

"Go away." He was getting more and more jittery by the second. "Interview's over, favor's done. Go away. Get outa the car."

I laid my left arm across his chest, holding him against the seat. My right hand patted him, didn't find anything that felt like a weapon. He was breathing hard, and looking all over the street like he expected tanks to show up any minute, but he didn't say anything.

I kept my left arm where it was, and thumbed the glove compartment. The door dropped down, and I took out the gun. I don't know guns, this was I guess a .32 caliber. It was a revolver, and stubby-barreled, all blue-black metal with a plain grip. The drum had places for six bullets. Two showed thin edges on each side, and those four had cartridges in them. I didn't know about the one in line with the barrel or the one underneath. Just above where my thumb naturally rested there was a little catch.

It pointed at S. I pushed it to O with my thumb, felt it click.

I took my left arm back, and half-turned in the seat, so I could face him and hold the gun in my lap aimed at him. He gave me a flying millisecond glance, eyed the street some more, and said, "I come to do a favor, that's all. Nothing else, nothing more. All bets are off. I don't say a word, you might's well get out of the car."

"Start the engine," I said.

He couldn't believe it. He wanted to know where I thought I was taking him.

"Home," I told him. "Binghamton's about a hundred thirty miles down 17. Drive."

"I won't do it," he said.

"Self-defense," I told him. "I wrestled the gun out of your hands. You were one of the men shot my father."

He stared at me. But he picked my right eye to stare at, the glass one. He shivered and started the car.

It was a long ride. We didn't talk much, and the highway looked too familiar. It was the same kind of situation, me in the same seat in the car. I kept looking back, and whenever a car passed us I winced, but nothing happened.

We made it in under four hours. We crossed the river on the first bridge, bypassing most of the town, but it was a little after four and rush-hour. It was slow going out to Vestal.

They built it up a lot in three years. The Penn-Can highway was going to bring civilization to the hometown after all. There were even split-level developments now, and ranch-style houses.

Bill lived in a ranch-style out on 26. There was nobody home when we got there, but the garage door was up and the car was out. I had the guy pull the Plymouth into the garage. We got out, and I switched the gun to my left hand again while he pulled the overhead door down. I'd been changing the gun back and forth from hand to hand about every half hour, when the fingers would start to cramp.

The door in the wall between the kitchen and the garage was also open, and the house was full of mosquitoes. The sink was full of dishes. The living-room floor was scattered with beer bottles and newspapers. Both were delivered, I guess. The beer bottles were twelve-ounce stubbies, the little fat ones you never see anywhere but at clambakes and sandlot ball games. There were two cases of them out in the garage and maybe a dozen cold in the refrigerator. That was practically all there was in the refrigerator.

The mosquitoes had the house to themselves. There were two bedrooms, and they were both empty. One had a crib and a white dresser and pink walls. The dresser drawers were open, empty. But Bill's clothes were all over the other bedroom and the closet, so he hadn't moved out. He was just boarding his kid with somebody, that's all. Probably Aunt Agatha.

We sat in the dinette and drank Bill's beer, and played gin with a deck of Bill's cards. The blue-black revolver looked strange on the rose-mottled formica of the table. The guy lost consistently. He couldn't keep his mind on the game. Every once in a while, he'd talk to me about letting him go. But he didn't really think he could convince me.

The backyard, just outside the dinette window, gradually became night. In the other direction, through the
archway, was the living room and the picture window. It
was night out that way, too, with a streetlight off a ways to
the side and amber light from the picture window across
the way.

Bill came home after ten. By the way he drove, he was
drunk. When he was in high school, he owned a Pontiac
with no back seat and a Mercury engine, and he shoved it
around tracks in stock races. Most of the time he was
drunk, and half the time he rode in the money. Sober, he
was a good hard driver. Drunk, he shaved his corners.

He came in wide-eyed, blue basketball jacket crooked
over T-shirt. He looked at me and shook his head and
leaned back against the kitchen wall. "Don't do that," he
said. His voice trembled. "Jesus, don't do that. I thought
it was Ann." He held a quaking hand to his chest.

It hadn't even occurred to me. Who but his wife would
be waiting home for him, the lights on? I got up, remem-
bering the gun just in time, and said, "I didn't think, Bill."

"Jesus," he said. He shook his head and licked his lips.
He pushed off from the wall and opened the refrigerator
door, and dropped the bottle he grabbed for. He shut the
door and fumbled for the bottle.

I thought he was going to fall over. I waved the gun at
my gin-partner. "Go open it for him," I said.

He did it. Bill watched him, frowning. He took the
bottle and drank from it, and then he said to me, "Who is
this?" He waved the bottle at the guy the way I'd waved
the gun.

"He met me outside the hospital," I said. I told the

27

story, finishing, "And he won't say any more than that."

"Oh, he won't." Bill put the bottle in his left hand, and hit the guy in the mouth.

I'd never seen that before, a man knocked out with one punch. The guy just fell down like his strings were cut.

I said, "That's bright. He'll talk a lot better in that condition."

"I didn't mean to hit him that hard." He gulped the beer again, put the bottle down on the drainboard, filled a glass with water.

"No," I said. I put the gun on top of the refrigerator, knelt beside the guy, slapped him awake. Over my shoulder, I said, "Make yourself some coffee. You're supposed to be three years older than me."

"I'm sorry," he said. "I'm sorry, Ray. I've been feeling sorry for myself."

"For how long?"

"I know. Two weeks ago today. Ann." He was on the verge of a crying jag.

"Make coffee," I said. "Three cups."

The guy on the floor twisted his head away from my slap. "Cut it out," he whined. "Cut it out."

"Get on your feet," I told him. "He won't hit you again."

He didn't believe me, but he got up, shakily. Bill was watching the water not boil. I said to him, "When you're sensible, come into the living room. Bring the coffee with you." I reached down the gun from the refrigerator.

Bill said, "I'm sorry, Ray. Jesus God, I'm sorry."

"If you start crying," I told him, "I'll walk out and the

hell with you." I prodded the guy into the living room. We turned on lights and sat looking across the street, where the picture window framed a happy family watching television, just like the ads in the *Saturday Evening Post*. It looked so normal I wanted to cry. Give me back my three years, Air Force. Four years, counting the year before they sent me to Germany. Give it back, I want to be home again, with Dad sometimes good for a game of catch, with Bill a big brother smelling of beer and Pontiac. I don't want to be twenty-three, without a home or an old man. I don't want a brother who's grieving for a wife I never even met. That makes us strangers.

I said to the guy, "What's your name?"

"Smitty."

"Crap."

"Honest to God. I got a library card to prove it."

That I wanted to see. Not to check the name, but because I wanted to see a library card that this guy would carry.

He showed it to me, and it was a Brooklyn library card. Typewritten, it said: Chester P. Smith, 653 East 99th St Local 36 Apt 2. Then there was a signature that might have been Chester P. Smith and might also have been Napoleon Bonaparte.

So he had a library card. In the same wallet he had forty-three dollars. But no driver's license, and I'd just been a hundred thirty miles in a car with him. "I'll call you Smitty," I said, tossing the wallet back, "but I bet Chester P. got mad when he had to go after a new card."

He put the wallet away. A couple minutes later, Bill

came in with three cups of coffee. Smitty shrank away when he brought the coffee over to him. Bill grinned like a spreading wound, and put the cup on the table beside the chair.

Bill and I sat on the sofa, and Smitty sat in the armchair near the picture window, half-facing us. After a minute, Bill said, "I'm okay now."

"Good," I said.

There was silence, and then Bill cleared his throat and said, "What are we waiting for?"

"Smitty to start talking," I said.

Smitty stuck a nervous thumb at the picture window. "Can't we close these drapes?"

"Do it yourself," I said.

He did, and sat down again, and looked miserable. He hunched over his knees and sipped coffee. Bill had made all three cups just black. We both drank it that way all the time. Smitty didn't like it, but he drank it.

"It's time to tell us the story, Smitty," I said.

"I can't," he said. He looked earnestly over the cup at us. "I come to do you a favor, pay back your old man. You rough me up. I should of stayed away in the first place."

I turned my head. "Bill, can you hit him any softer than the last time? I hate waking him up all the time."

Bill got up, eager, grinning. He wanted to even the slate. "I've got some beauties in here," he said, and showed us his right fist. It had red hair and orange freckles all over it. The knuckles were big.

Smitty said, "Come on. Lay off me, come on." His voice was higher. He was pushing back down in the chair.

"Tell us an easy part first," I said. "What was the favor my father did you?"

His eyes were on Bill's fist. "It was before you were born," he said. "Before repeal. I was driving a truckload in from New Hampshire when the state boys got me."

"A truckload of what?" Bill asked him.

"Whiskey." He would have said it with contempt for Bill's ignorance, but he still had respect for Bill's fist. "The people I worked for threw me away, but your old man was my mouthpiece. For no dough."

"How did he know you?" I asked.

"We worked for the same people."

Bill took a step toward him. "That's a lie."

"Wait," I said. "Okay, Smitty, now the current events."

"I told you the whole thing. There's gonna be trouble in New York. You don't want any part of it."

"I want every part of it," I told him. "Names and addresses. They killed my father." I pointed at Bill. "They killed his wife."

He looked surprised, for just a second. Then his face closed up again, and he said, "Okay, right there that tells you."

"Tells me what?"

"Why you ought to clear out."

"Because Bill's wife was killed?"

"You don't want to be involved."

"I *am* involved, whether I like it or not. Tell me about this trouble that's going to happen in New York."

He hesitated, considering, looking from me to Bill and back. Then he said, "It's got to do with the Organization. That's all I'll say, that's too much already."

"What organization?"

"The mob. The outfit. The syndicate, you might call it."

"What do I have to do with the syndicate?"

"On account of your father."

"What does he have to do with it?"

"He used to work for it."

Bill went over and hit him twice before I could move. Then I got to him and pulled him away. I said, "Control yourself, goddamn you to hell, or I take him away and you can screw yourself. You want to cry in your beer, or do you want to help?"

"All right, all *right*." He pulled away from me and went over and sat on the sofa again.

Smitty had protected himself with his arms. He lowered them now like they ached. His eyes were round. He said, "*I* didn't do it. What's the matter with him? I come to do you a favor. What's the matter with him?"

"He lost a wife."

"It wasn't *me.* I come to warn you. I should of stayed away in the first place."

I said, "Who did it, Smitty? Who killed my father? Who killed Bill's wife?"

He shook his head. "No. You two are crazy. You'll go after them, and they'll trace it back to me. I just come to do you a friendly gesture. Because of your old man. I don't want to get killed."

"What are their names, Smitty?"

"They'll trace it back to me. I don't talk any more."

I said, "Bill."

It was a long night. We kept the drapes shut. Bill

knocked him out and I woke him up. But there was somebody in the world who could scare Smitty more from a distance than we could close up. The last time, I didn't wake him. We dumped him in a closet and locked the door and went to sleep.

Four

In the morning, before we left, Bill wanted to do something nutty like bury him in the cellar or leave him on a side road in his own car and with a bullet in his head from his own gun. "If we let him live," he argued, "he'll go right back and let them know we're coming."

"No, he won't," I said. I looked at Smitty and talked to Bill. "He'll have to tell them he talked to us. They won't believe he didn't give names. So he won't go back to New York at all."

"No," he said. "I won't." His words were slurred, because of his puffed lips.

"He'll go west some place," I said, "and change his name."

He caught the quote. He said, "You won't ever hear from me again."

After a while, Bill took my word for it, and moved his Mercury out of the driveway. Smitty backed his Plymouth out and drove away. He didn't pause to ask directions.

Bill had to go into town and say goodbye to his boss and his kid, and get his money out of the bank. I stayed behind and packed suitcases and locked the windows. When he came back, we loaded the trunk and headed for New York.

I was still shaky in the right-hand seat. I tried driving for a while, but it was too hard. Not only the distance judgment, also the right ankle. They hadn't been able to fix it completely. It wouldn't bend any more, and made me gimp a little. I had to push the accelerator down with my heel, and it was awkward. So we switched again, and Bill drove the rest of the way. We went down through Pennsylvania, 11 and Carbondale and 106 and the Delaware Water Gap. It was the same distance, and 17 made us leery.

We went down Jersey and over the bridge to Staten Island and across Staten Island and over the new bridge to Brooklyn. Then we went up the Belt Parkway and through the tunnel into Manhattan.

We'd kept Smitty's revolver. Bill had a Luger that maybe still worked, but no ammunition for it. He'd tried in Binghamton, but neither he nor the clerk was sure what size cartridge it wanted. He was going to try again in New York. Also in the trunk we had two deer rifles.

We got a hotel way up Broadway, 72nd Street, fairly cheap with a garage. Bill had almost four thousand dollars. I had not quite a hundred. The Air Force had sent the second hundred of my mustering-out pay to the hospital. God knew where the third hundred would go. That should be coming soon. Next Monday I'd be out two months. That seemed hard to believe.

It was only a little after two when we checked in. Bill found a bank a couple blocks down from the hotel. He put three grand in a joint checking account. We both signed cards and got a checkbook. They were unhappy. They wanted to give us one with our names on the checks.

After lunch, we went back to the room and sat on the beds. Bill said, "Now what?"

I said, "We go in two directions. The license plate of Smitty's car is one. But I think that was probably stolen. The other is Dad. He was a lawyer in New York, way back when. He had something to do with the underworld."

"That's a lie. That punk was lying."

"No. It's something from that time that killed him. They were looking for him, maybe. He figured it was safe to come to New York, after all these years. But he was nervous about going out of the hotel."

"But why Ann?"

"Tell me about that."

"She was in the Civic Theater. You know, amateur. She spent two, three evenings a week at rehearsals. She'd take the bus in and get somebody to drive her back. I couldn't go get her on account of Betsy. And the bus doesn't run that late. That night, she took the bus in like always. It was three blocks to walk to where they rehearsed. She was cross-c-crossing the street. It wasn't even dark, it was only seven-thirty. Early evening. The car came ou-came out of the side street, clipped her. She got kno-knocked—"

"Okay," I said. "Take it easy. You don't have to tell me now."

"I'll get it over with," he said. He lit a cigarette. "Back onto the sidewalk," he said. "The car knocked her back-back—"

"Okay."

"Jesus." He breathed loudly, inhale and exhale, staring at the bedspread pattern. He laid his hand on the bedspread, fingers splayed out. He pressed down and said, "Three people saw it. Nobody saw it clear. The car didn't even slow down."

I said, "I wonder if it was the same car."

He looked at me. "As went after you?"

"Uh huh."

"I don't know. I suppose so. Nobody saw it clear."

He finished his cigarette. I went over to the phone, and looked at the directories. They had the Manhattan and the Brooklyn and the Bronx. I found Chester P. Smith in the Brooklyn book, at 653 East 99th Street. Nightingale 9-9970.

A woman answered. I asked for Smitty, and she said, "Who?"

"Chet. Chester."

"He's at work. Who is this?"

"I think we were in the service together," I said. "If this is the right Chester Smith. Medium height, thin-faced."

She laughed, as though she were mad. "There's nothing thin about *this* Chester," she said.

"Can't be the same guy," I said.

I hung up and looked for the public library in the Manhattan directory. It said there was a Newspaper Division at 521 West 43. I said, "I'm going out for a while."

Bill said, "Where?"

"Library. You could figure out how we check that license plate."

"What the hell you doing at the library?"

"I want to see if Dad ever made the paper."

"You mean with the underworld? Bootleggers?" He got to his feet, frowning and mad. "That punk was lying, Ray. What kind of a son are you?"

"A son with his last eye open," I said.

He hung fire, and then turned away. "Hell," he said. "I haven't been getting any sleep."

"I'll be back after a while."

He flung himself face down on his bed and I left the room.

Five

It was between Tenth and Eleventh Avenue. That whole block was sewing machine wholesalers. The newspaper library was the second floor of a building that looked like a post office. Some papers they had on microfilm, some they had bound in big books.

I looked through the *New York Times Index*. I found it in 1931. Dad was only twenty-seven then. He was married, but he didn't have any kids yet. He'd been a lawyer two years.

There was a guy, he owned a lot of buildings. Most of them were tenements, slum buildings. Almost all of them had speak-easies in them. He was up for allowing liquor to be stored and sold on his property with his knowledge. He got off on a brilliant piece of legal footwork on the part of his lawyer, a member of the firm of McArdle,

Lamarck & Krishman. It was so brilliant the *Times* did a profile on the lawyer, whose name was Willard Kelly, and on the firm he worked for.

McArdle, Lamarck & Krishman, "it was alleged," got virtually all of their business, directly or indirectly, from the liquor syndicate. Willard Kelly had been with the firm less than a year. This was the first time he'd handled a case in court for them. The profile writer was sad that Kelly was selling his brilliance to the underworld.

Your father. You think you know him. You forget he lived a lot of years before he started you. All of a sudden you find out you never knew who the hell he was.

I wrote down all the names. Morris Silber, the landlord. Andrew McArdle and Philip Lamarck and Samuel Krishman, partners in the law firm. George Ellinbridge, the prosecuting attorney. Andrew Shuffleman, the judge.

Willard Kelly didn't show up again. I went back through the *Index*, twenties and thirties, checking the other names. Morris Silber got a year in jail in 1937 for housing violations in his tenements, mainly rats. His lawyer wasn't named. Philip Lamarck died in bed in 1935, at the age of sixty-seven. Andrew Shuffleman died just as peaceably the same year, at the age of seventy-one. George Ellinbridge was elected State Assemblyman in 1938, but wasn't re-elected.

Andrew McArdle personally defended crime kingpin Anthony Edward "Eddie" Kapp in his income-tax evasion trial in 1940. The crime kingpin went to jail, with two sentences of ten years and one of five years, to run consecutively and *not* concurrently. Twenty-five years. It wasn't up yet, but there were such things as paroles.

Eddie Kapp. I didn't find any references to him later than 1940. I found a lot of them in the early thirties and late twenties. A friend of Dutch Schultz and Bill Bailey. An important man around that crazy time when Schultz was killed over in Jersey and Bailey became top man for two weeks. Then Bailey walked into a New York City hospital one afternoon and said he didn't feel well. They put him to bed, and two o'clock the following morning he was dead. The death certificate said pneumonia.

Eddie Kapp. Willard Kelly. Connected by a man named Andrew McArdle.

I wasted some time, then, looking in the current year's *Index*. They had monthly indices in a filler book, and July was the most recent. My name was there, for July 14th. I filled out a slip, got the microfilm, and put it in the viewer. I read about the shooting. The *Times* called it "bizarre." It only rated a small paragraph on page eight. DRIVER SHOT AT WHEEL.

The woman came over and told me it was five o'clock, closing time. I put the microfilm back in the box, put my pencil and pad in my pocket, and left.

Six

Back at the room, there was a guy with Bill. He had on a brown suit with the coat open. His white shirt was bunched at the waist. He was thin and his tie was brown

39

and orange and green and he wore a brown hat back on his head indoors.

Bill said, "This is Ed Johnson. He's a private detective."

Johnson grinned at me. "That's right," he said.

I frowned at Bill. "What the hell for?"

"We're not going to get anywhere on our own. You got some jerky idea about Dad mixed up with the underworld. We need somebody who knows the ropes."

I looked at Johnson. "Get out," I said.

His grin faded. "Well, I don't know," he said. He looked from me to Bill to me. "I've been given a retainer, to check out a license plate."

"We want to do that," Bill told me.

I sat down and lit a cigarette. "We don't want to spread our business around," I told the match. "We don't want to finger ourselves."

"I'm trustworthy," Johnson told me. "One hundred per cent."

"Just the license, Ray," said Bill. He sounded embarrassed.

Johnson said, "You couldn't do it, I can."

I shrugged. "The hell with it," I said. "Go play with the license plate. It was on a Plymouth."

He looked from face to face again, and then he said he'd be seeing us, and left.

Bill said, "That was a hell of a way to talk. He's a nice guy."

I said, "He's a stranger."

"We need somebody dispassionate. You've got this nutty idea—"

I took out the pad and read aloud from it. Then I tossed it on the dresser and said, "Smarten up."

Bill pushed words into the silence like a man pushing logs into mud. "It wasn't Dad. Willard Kelly, that isn't an uncommon name. Hell, it's *my* name, too."

"Just a coincidence."

"Sure."

"Two Willard Kellys. Both the same age. Both in New York. Both lawyers. Both graduates of the same school."

"Maybe. Why not?"

"You ought to go back to Binghamton, Bill. You're blind in both eyes. You'll get us in a lot of trouble."

He looked at me, and then he went and sat on the bed. He sat in the middle of the bed, knees folded like a yogi. He looked big and pathetic. His blunt fingers, hairy and freckled, traced the pattern of the spread.

After a while, he said, "My *father.*"

A while longer and he said, "He wasn't like that."

"He changed. Reformed. Quit the syndicate and moved away."

His eyes had sad, shredded edges. "That's true?"

"Something like that."

"That was really him, in the paper?"

"You know it."

He made a fist and pounded the pattern. "How the hell can I have any *respect* for him?"

I popped the eye out and got to my feet. I put it on the dresser and said, "Get up, Bill."

He was puzzled. "Why?"

"You lose respect too easy."

"I don't want to fight you, Ray."

41

He came off the bed with his hands spread, and I hit him on the side of the jaw.

The third time I hit him, he swung back. I was at a disadvantage, I didn't always judge the distance right. I walked into a few. I kept getting up. He started to cry, and his face was as red as his hair, and he kept knocking me down again. Then he put his hands at his sides and shook his head and whispered, "No more." I got up and hit him with my left hand. He didn't dodge or raise his arms or defend himself or fight back. I hit him with the right hand. And the left hand again. He blubbered, "No more." I hit him right hand and then left hand. He dropped to his knees, and the vibration knocked the Gideon Bible off the nightstand. I hit him right hand, from the knees coming up, and he went over on his back. He wouldn't get up.

I got the eye from the dresser and went into the head. I washed my face and watched myself put the eye in. It didn't make me want to throw up any more. My knuckles were scraped and there was a ragged cut on the left side of my jaw.

I went back and sat down in the chair again. After a while, Bill sat up. He said, "All right."

I said, "You going back to Binghamton?"

"No. You're right."

I wasn't sure he knew. I said, "Why did you think I came here? To play Summer Festival?"

"No," he said. "I know that."

"Do you know what we're doing here?"

"Yes."

"What?"

"We're looking for the people who killed Dad."

"For the cops?"

He looked at me. "Jesus," he said. He shook his head and looked away. "No," he said. "Not for the cops."

"For us," I said. "Why?"

He looked at me level this time. "Because he was our father."

"That's right," I said.

Seven

We spent the evening in the room, with separate bottles of Old Mr. Boston. Johnson woke us on the phone at nine in the morning. I talked to him. He said, "Those plates are registered to a '54 Buick. Stolen three months ago. Not the car, just the plates. Lots of Plymouths stolen. It's a popular car."

I said, "Thanks. The retainer cover it?"

"If that's all you want," he said.

"Thanks," I said.

"Listen, Mr. Kelly, you don't have to dislike me."

"I don't dislike you." I hung up and forgot him. I spent a few minutes with the phone directory and a pencil, and then we went out to eat.

It was now McArdle, Krishman, Mellon & McArdle. It was a building on the east side of Fifth Avenue, just down a ways from the cathedral. Friday morning, the early tourists streamed north to look at the cathedral and the Plaza. We pushed across their path from the cab to the doors. The tourist ladies wore green cotton dresses. All the little boys had hats like Daddy's. I gave mine up when I was twelve. It was a Sunday hat, for church. I never wore it in New York. Lots of people don't take their kids to New York. It doesn't mean anything.

The elevator had chrome doors on the first floor. On the twenty-seventh, they were metal doors painted maroon. A clever sign-painter had fit the whole name of the law firm on the frosted glass of the door. We went in and I asked the girl for Mr. McArdle. "The first one," I said. She acted snooty, like a whole dancing class at once. She gave us the second one.

He was about forty, with a soft body and a pale round face. His eyes were wet behind black-armored spectacles. "Well, boys," he said. "What can I do for you?"

"Nothing," I said. "We want McArdle number one."

"My father isn't an active part of the firm any more." He smiled, like a man selling laxative. "I assure you, I'm almost as good a lawyer as he."

He was playing us for teenagers. I said, "Sure. We'll take Krishman. Samuel Krishman. Not a coat-tail relation."

He frowned, mouth and eyebrows both. "I'm afraid I'll have to ask you—"

"Tell him Willard Kelly," I said.

It didn't mean anything to him. He looked down at the card on his desk. "You gave your first name as Raymond."

"That's my father."

"Raymond is your father?"

"You're a goddamn imbecile, mister." I pointed at the phone. "Pick it up and tell Samuel Krishman Willard Kelly's son is here."

"I'll do no such thing."

I went over and picked up the phone. He reached for it and I said, "Bill." He looked at Bill, who was coming around the desk, and he sat back, paler than before. "You won't get away with this," he said. But he was gabbling. It was just a sentence you say when people push you around and get away with it.

There was a row of buttons on the phone, under the dial. I pushed the one that said, "Local." Nothing happened. I dialed zero. Still nothing happened. I dialed some other number, I don't know what. A guy came on and I said, "What the hell is Samuel's number? I can't remember."

"Eight," he said.

I broke the connection and dialed eight. An old man came on. I said, "I'm Willard Kelly's son. I'm not as dumb as Andrew McArdle's son, but I'm stuck in his office."

There was a pause, and the dry old voice said, "What was that name?"

"You heard it right. Willard Kelly."

"Is Lester there?"

"McArdle two? Yes."

"Tell him to show you to my office."

"Tell him yourself. He won't believe me."

I straight-armed Lester the phone. He took it like it had bitten him once. He listened and agreed and hung up and said to me, "You could have been more civil."

"Not to you."

He showed us down a corridor that was green on one wall, rust on the other. White ceiling, black linoleum. Pastel doors. The one at the end was tan and closed and didn't say anything. He handed us to a girdled brunette with a plaster hairdo. She played electronically and let us in.

When I was a kid I believed in a Business Pope. I thought there was a strict mercantile hierarchy, grocery stores and movie houses down near the bottom, factories and warehouses in the middle, Wall Street up near the top. And a Business Pope running the whole thing. I visualized the Business Pope as a shriveled ancient white-haired Pluto in a black leather chair. Black-capped chauffeur to the left, white-hipped nurse to the right. Every line on his face would record a decade of evil and cruelty and decay. I knew just what he would look like.

That was Samuel Krishman. No chauffeur and no nurse. Black leather swivel chair. A mahogany desk of wood so warm it glowed. Maroon desk blotter. Two black telephones. Discreet papers, embarrassed to be white.

He said, "Pardon me for not rising." Five words he could say without thinking about them, while studying us. He waved a gnarled root of a hand at two maroon leather chairs. His cuff links were round, gold coins with Roman profiles.

He looked at me. "You say you're Willard Kelly's son?"

"We both are. That's Willard Junior. I'm Raymond."

The pale eyes flicked to Bill and back to me. "You're spokesman. You're the one who spoke on the phone." That was easy. I was looking at him, Bill was looking at me.

I said, "My father used to work here."

He smiled. The perfect false teeth couldn't have looked more out of place in a duck's mouth. "Not here, precisely. Our offices were farther downtown then."

"He went to work for you in August of 1930."

"I suppose so. Approximately."

"He made the *Times* once, on the Morris Silber case. They did a profile."

The smile this time didn't part the lips. It looked healthier. "I remember that. Willard was embarrassed. A shy young man. Unlike his son." By him, Bill wasn't even there.

"He made the *Times* again," I said. "Two months ago. You didn't see it?"

Thin eyebrows crawled on the rutted forehead. "Not that I recall. I didn't notice it, perhaps." The smile was open-mouthed again. "I read little beyond the obituary page these days."

I had the system now. When he showed his teeth the smile was phony. I said, "This wasn't the obituary page, but it was the same thing. He was killed."

"Killed?"

"Shot. In a moving car, by a moving car. I was with him."

"Ah. Did you recognize the attacker?"

"I will."

"I see." His hands crept up on the maroon blotter, crawled blindly together, clung. "That's why you're here," he said. "You want vengeance."

"Second," I said. "First, I want understanding. I was away for three years. Air Force. Germany. I just came back. No girl yet, no plans yet." I jabbed a thumb at Bill. "He was out of it. Married, with a kid. All I had was home, and all that was was Dad. Twenty-three years and they left us alone. When I needed him most, they came

47

in. Arrogant. *Grinning*." I sat there. We were all quiet. I took my hands off the wooden chair-arms. The palms had the red lines of the wood. "I want to know why," I said.

"They killed my wife," said Bill. It was a truculent apology for being there.

Krishman sighed, and rubbed his face with one dry hand. He wasn't the Business Pope, he was just an old man, afraid to retire because his friends died when they retired. "That was all so many years ago," he said. "That's behind us now. We don't have things like that any more."

"Anastasia," I said. "The Victor Reisel blinding. Arnold Schuster, the twenty-two-year-old witness got killed in 1951."

"This firm," he said, "hasn't been involved for nearly twenty years. There were circumstances…"

"McArdle number one?"

He shook his head. He looked at me and smiled with closed lips. "Philip Lamarck," he said. "His name came second, but he was the senior partner."

"He died in '35."

"It takes a while to break free of connections like that."

"When did you break free?"

"Shortly before the war. 1940, I suppose."

"Was Dad still working for you?"

"He left us around then. Left the city, I believe."

"That was the year of the Eddie Kapp trial, wasn't it?"

"Eddie Kapp? Oh, yes, the income-tax trial. It's been a very long time, you must understand…"

"Is he out yet?"

"Kapp? I have no idea. You think there's a connection between him and your father's death?"

"When he was shot, Dad said his name. 'Kapp,' that's all."

"Are you sure that's what he meant?"

"No. But it's likely. Would McArdle know?"

"Know what?"

"If Kapp was out yet."

"I doubt it. You want to talk to him, I suppose."

"Yes."

He nodded. "I'll call him. I'm sure he'll talk to you. We all liked Willard very much. A brilliant legal mind, for such a young man. And a cheerful red-headed Irishman." He nodded at Bill. "You look very much like him." Back to me. "You take after Edith more. The fair hair, shape of your face."

I suppose so.

"From what you've said, I take it your mother is dead."

"Died when I was two. In Binghamton."

"That's where he went. He should have stayed in New York. His talents would be wasted anywhere else. Corporation law, but with fine courtroom presence."

"He did corporate work in Binghamton. Small-time. You say you've got a different class of client now?"

"Yes. Since before the war. Shipping lines, food packagers. Industrial corporations almost exclusively."

"McArdle handled the Kapp income-tax case, didn't he?"

"Yes, I believe he did."

"Did my father have anything to do with that case?"

"I should think so. He had the Kapp file."

"What?"

"He was the one who normally handled all of Kapp's legal affairs. You see, every regular continuous client has a file, kept by the man in this office who is his immediate contact and who does all or most of his legal work. The income-tax trial, of course, was something else again. Not that Willard Kelly couldn't have handled it as well as anybody. But Kapp was an important client at the time. It was necessary to have one of the firm's partners in charge of the case."

"Who were Dad's other regular clients?"

"I'm sure I have no idea."

"What about the files?"

He shook his head. "Some files," he said, "we retain for seven years, some for fifteen years, a few for twenty. We would have no files at all for that far back. Your father left us more than twenty years ago."

"If you had the same kind of client that you have now, would you have the files?"

Closed-lips smile. "Most likely."

"What about Morris Silber?"

"Is that the case when the *Times* wrote the profile?"

"Yes."

"I'm sorry. He was minor even then. I would have no idea where he is today or if he's even still alive."

"But Dad had his file."

"Yes, of course."

"Can you think of anyone else?"

Parted-lips smile, hands spread out, trembling a bit at the end of his sleeves. "It's been so long."

"Sure. You said you'd call McArdle one."

"Of course."

He spent a few minutes on the phone. He called McArdle 'Andrew,' not Andy or anything like that. He didn't say anything surprising. When he hung up he said, "Do you have a car?"

Bill spoke for the second time. "Yes."

Krishman told him, "He lives out on the Island. Long Island. Beyond King's Park, on the North Shore. He has an estate out there." He gave Bill directions, route numbers and so on, and Bill nodded. Then we got up to leave. I thanked him for his answers, he congratulated Dad on producing such fine boys.

At the door, I turned and said, "Up till 1940, when you made the changeover, about how many professional criminals did you help evade the law?"

"I have no idea."

"More than a hundred?"

Closed-lips smile. "Oh, yes. Far more."

"Aren't you afraid of the retribution of justice?"

"At this late date? Hardly."

"You will never be punished by the law."

"Never. I'm sure of it."

"And you obviously haven't lost your money or your social standing. Do you have ulcers, or anything like that?"

"No. I'm perfectly healthy. My doctor says I'll live past ninety. Do you have a point to make?"

"Yes. To my brother, not to you. He needs an education. He still believes in good guys and bad guys. That they're born that way and stay that way. And that good guys always win and bad guys always lose."

Closed-lips smile. "A great number of people believe that. It's comforting to them."

I said, "Until the guns come out."

Eight

It was forty miles out to McArdle's place. We took the Triborough Bridge and the Expressway. For the first ten or fifteen miles it was all city, slit open by the Expressway. After Floral Park and Mineola it got more suburb. Every once in a while, there was a glimpse of Long Island Sound off to our left. But it still didn't seem any more like an island than Manhattan did.

The last mile and a half was private road, blacktop. McArdle shared it with two other millionaires, and his place was last of the three, where the road made a hangman's knot. There was a birdbath inside the loop, and a Negro with a power mower. The house was clapboard and brick and masonry. Windows enclosed the porch.

When we got out of the car, the Negro stopped and wiped his face with a white handkerchief. His hat was gray and he held it in his left hand, then put it back on his head. He kept the power mower running, and it sounded loud but far away, the way they do. He never quite looked at us, and he never quite looked away.

We went up the stoop and tried the screen door. It was locked and there wasn't any bell. I rattled the door and shouted. A guy in a white jacket came out, carrying a towel. He looked at us through the screen.

"Kelly," I said. "We're expected."

He pointed to his right. "Down at the dock," he said. He went back inside.

The house was backed against a half-moon of forest. A brown path led in among the trees to the left of the house, going gradually downhill. We went down it. Behind us, the Negro put his handkerchief away and went back to work.

A voice droned ahead. The path wound downhill. Through the trees, there were blue glimpses of the Sound.

We came out on a narrow strip of shade-mottled lawn. At the lower end, a swath of smooth pebbles led down into the water. A little blond girl in a ruffled bathing suit stood half-bent in the shallows, filling her green pail with water.

The lawn was flanked by brush and trees, down the sides and overhanging the water's edge. To the right, an unpainted dock jutted out atilt into the water. A white motorboat nodded beside it. A boy and girl of about twenty were on and off a float a ways away. Four people sat in white-fence lawn chairs to the right, three of them watching the little girl.

The woman of about twenty-seven, with the white bathing suit and the ash-blond hair and the vertical frown lines between her brows, would be the mother of the little girl and the sister of one or both of the people out on the float. The nondescript middle-aged heavy couple in city clothes would be her parents, he the brother of the McArdle I'd met at the law office, this one older and tougher and not a lawyer. The gross ancient bald man wearing young man's sports clothes would be Andrew McArdle.

I stopped and looked at him. The short-sleeved white shirt showed flabby blue-veined white-skinned arms, the muscles so little able to bear weight that the upper slopes of the arms were only skin over narrow frail bone, the fat all hanging in long bags of skin underneath. The shirt was open at the throat, showing gray flesh writhing over a convulsive Adam's apple. There was no chest. The shirt sagged down to a gross belly. Tan slacks covered the stick legs beneath, and the feet were bare, looking like frozen plaster molds.

His head sagged back, his mouth hung open, the thin-veined lids were stretched over his eyes. The sound of his breathing was very loud.

The voice I'd heard had been the middle-aged man. He stopped and looked at us. The women turned their heads and looked, and then the ash-blonde watched the little girl again. The boy and girl on the float stood still, arms at their sides, gazing in at us. The little girl ignored us. She laughed suddenly and splashed herself with water.

The ancient man gulped and rolled his head around and opened his eyes. He stared at Bill. "Willard." His voice was a croak that had once been a ringing bass.

I came across the lawn, Bill trailing me. "Mr. Krishman called you," I said.

The present slowly came into his eyes. He looked at me. "Yes. Arthur, go up to the house. All of you, up to the house."

The middle-aged woman smiled like a beautician. "You shouldn't exert yourself, Papa." She got up and crouched over him, hoping everyone would think she was solicitous. She was afraid to strangle him. "Don't you talk too long, now," she said.

Arthur said to her, "Come on."

The ash-blonde called to the little girl, "Linda. Come here."

She came out of the water, carrying the green pail. She stopped in front of me, serious, squinting up at me with sun in her eyes. "Why do you limp?"

"I was in an accident."

"When?"

"Come along, Linda," said her mother.

"Two months ago," I said.

"Where?"

"Your mother wants you."

They trailed by us, across the lawn toward the path. The middle-aged woman said, "I'm *coming*, Arthur."

They trailed diagonally up the lawn. The last thing, the ash-blonde made the little girl empty the water out of her pail. Then they were gone, between the trees.

He told us to sit down, and we did. He kept his head back, twisted at an odd angle on a faded flower-pattern pillow. His voice was just above a whisper, no louder than his breathing. "Your father is dead," he said.

I said, "I want to know about Eddie Kapp."

"He went to jail. Years ago." The head shook back and forth, slowly. "The Federal Government is a different proposition, Eddie."

"Is he still in jail? Eddie Kapp, is he still in jail?"

"Oh, I suppose so. I don't know. I have taken the final sabbatical, young man. I am no longer chained to the office, I—" His wandering eyes and wandering mind touched Bill again, and he frowned. "Willard? You shouldn't be here, you know that."

Bill was scared. He said, "No, you mean my father." He broke the mood before McArdle said anything useful.

McArdle's face started to close up. He was in the present again, and he remembered what he'd said. He watched me warily.

I said, "Why shouldn't he be here?"

"Who? What are you talking about? I am retired, an old man with a bad heart..."

"My father shouldn't have come to New York, should he? Why not?"

"I don't know. My memory wanders sometimes, I'm not always responsible for what I say."

The boy and girl came dripping out of the water. McArdle's head twisted to glare at them. "Go out there! Stay out there! This is none of your business!"

"We're going up to the house," said the girl. She was snotty. She'd had money all her life, she didn't care if she inherited or not. "Come on, Larry."

They paused to fiddle with towels and cigarettes and sunglasses. I said, "Better hurry."

The girl was going to be snotty to me, but then she wasn't. She grabbed her gear and hip-jiggled away. She looked discontented, frustrated. The boy flexed his muscles at me, frowning because he'd been left out, and followed her.

When they were gone, I turned back to McArdle. "Who would know if Eddie Kapp was out or in?"

"I don't know. So long ago." The eyes misted again,

cleared a little. "Maybe his sister. Dorothea. She married a chain-market manager."

"What name?"

"I'm trying to remember. Carter, something like that. Castle, Kimball... Campbell! That was it, Robert Campbell."

I wrote it down. "That was in New York?"

"He managed a chain market in Brooklyn. A Bohack? I don't remember. A young man. She was young, too, much younger than her brother. A pretty thing, black hair. Glowing."

He was starting to dream again. I said, "Who told Willard Kelly to stay out of town?"

"What? What?" His head nearly raised up from the pillow, and then subsided. "Don't shout so," he said. His breathing was louder. "I am an old man, my memory is failing me, I have a bad heart. You cannot rely on what I say. I should have told Samuel no. I should have refused."

"Samuel Krishman? He doesn't know the answer, does he?"

The belly laughed, shaking him. "He never knew anything. A fool!"

"But you do."

He started the old man routine again. I said, "Tell me who told Willard Kelly to stay out of town."

"I don't know."

"Who told Willard Kelly to stay out of town?"

"Go away. I don't know."

"Who told Willard Kelly to stay out of town?"

"No. No!"

I kept my voice low. "Tell me or I'll kill you."

"I'm an old man—"

"You'll die. Here and now."

"Let me go. Let the past alone!"

I bowed my head, covered my face with my hands. I plucked the glass oval out. I closed my left eye, and then I was blind. I kept the right lid open, but it was a strain with the eye out. It was warm in my palm.

I lowered my hands in my lap. Still blind, I raised my face toward him. I smiled. "I can see your soul this way," I said. "It's black."

I heard a choking. I opened my eye and he was gaping, staring, choking, his face turning bluish red. I put the glass eye back in.

Bill was already running up the path, shouting for the family.

Nine

I had meant to frighten him. He was afraid of death, and I think he would have answered me. I had no idea how strongly it would affect him. I hadn't meant him to die.

We had to stay and wait for the doctor. I told them our father had once worked for McArdle, Lamarck & Krishman. I told them he had died recently, but I didn't tell them how. I told them he had told us once to look up his old bosses, they could maybe help us get a start in life.

They believed me. It was believable. Bill listened to

me tell it, and then he knew it too. But he wasn't meeting my glance. He thought I'd done it on purpose. I'd have to tell him, once we got away from here.

While we waited, I talked with Karen Thorndike. She was the ash-blonde. She was the daughter of Arthur and the woman with the beautician's smile, as I'd supposed. She was divorced from Jerry Thorndike. She said, "You don't want to come to New York."

"Why not?"

"There's nothing here but people clawing each other. Everybody wants to get to the top of the heap, and it's a heap of human beings. A big hill of kicking, struggling human beings, trying to crawl up one another and be at the top."

"You're thinking of Jerry Thorndike," I said. "You got burned. Not all the people in a city are like that."

"They are in New York."

Linda, the little girl, came over and started asking stupid questions. She was like her mother, interesting until she opened her mouth. I thought of taking my eye out for her, but not seriously.

The doctor was big and hearty. People paid him to be like him. His name was Heatherton. He wanted to know what we'd been talking about when the old man had had his attack. I said the weather in New York.

Nobody was really upset. He was eighty-two years old. They'd all been hanging around waiting anyway. After a while, I asked Dr. Heatherton if there was any reason for Bill and me to stay there any longer. He said no.

As we went out the private road, a gray Cadillac hearse purred by us, going in.

It wasn't yet three. But it was Friday afternoon, so there was quite a bit of traffic headed toward the city, most of it in late-model cars.

We rode in silence for a while, and then I lit a cigarette and handed it out to Bill and he said, "No, thanks," without looking away from the road.

I stuck the cigarette back between my lips and said, "Don't be stupid. I didn't want to kill him."

"You said you were going to." He glowered grimly at the road. "You told him you would and you did. I don't know you any more, the Air Force did something to you. Or Germany."

"Or being in the car with Dad."

"All right, maybe that. Whatever caused it, I don't like it. You can have the money in the bank. I'll need the car, I'm going back to Binghamton."

"You don't care any more."

"I'll stop off and talk to that state cop, Kirk."

"And tell him what?"

"I won't tell him anything. Don't worry, I'm not going to inform on you."

"I'm not worried."

"I'm going to ask him how they're doing."

"They aren't doing. Tuesday it'll be two months. They don't have a lead, a clue, a chance, or a hope. If they did, it wouldn't take two months. It's us or nobody."

"I can't stay with you. I can't be around you, with you pulling things like that."

"I told you, that was a mistake. I didn't mean for him to die."

"Sure."

"You're a cluck, Bill. You're three years older than me, but you're a cluck. He knew who chased Dad out of town. Did you hear what he said?"

"I heard him."

"He *knew*. Do you think I wanted him dead?"

He frowned at the wheel, thinking it over. After a while he glanced at me. I looked innocent. He glowered out at the highway again. "Then what the hell did you do it for?"

"I was trying to scare him. I didn't know it would hit him that big. It must look pretty bad."

In some out-of-the-way corner he found a grin. He took it out, dusted it off, put it on his face. It looked good there. "You don't know how bad, Ray," he said. "I about had a heart attack myself. You looked like something out of hell." He glanced at me again, back at the traffic. "A little worse than usual," he said.

"You want a cigarette?"

"I need one," he said.

We went back to the hotel and sat around. We went out for dinner and bought some more Old Mr. Boston. We drank and smoked and talked and played gin a penny a point. He won.

After a while, we finished the booze and went to bed and turned the lights off. But I saw McArdle's face, bluish red, the eyes bulging bigger and bigger. I got up and told Bill I was going out. He was asleep already, and he just grunted.

I went out and it was one o'clock in the morning. No liquor stores open. I found a bar, but the only thing he'd sell me to go was beer. I had five fast Fleischmann doubles on the rocks, and then I bought two quarts of Rheingold beer and brought them back to the room. I knew they'd make me throw up and they did, but after that I could go to sleep.

Ten

Johnson was around in the morning again. He wanted to talk. I had a split head, I told him to wait. He sat smoking in a chair while Bill and I hulked around and washed our faces and got dressed. Then the three of us went out for coffee.

We went up Broadway to a Bickford's, and filled our trays. Johnson just had coffee. Bill and I had eggs.

At the table, Johnson stuck a spoon in his coffee and stirred for five minutes without paying any attention, while he talked. "I want to give you a little background on me," he said. "I run a one-man agency. Maybe one or two jobs a month, enough to stay even with the bills. Last year I made thirty-seven hundred dollars. I hate the job, I don't know why I stay in. Same way a little grocer down the block from the A&P won't close up and go get a warehouse job. You keep waiting for something to happen, like in the paperbacks."

He held the spoon against the side of the cup with his thumb and drank. The spoon handle jabbed into his cheek. He kept watching me while he drank. Then he said, "Most of the time, it's sitting around waiting for that one or two jobs a month. It's boring as hell. So sometimes I get interested in something. Like you two. Upstate accents, with the broad A, and you're living in a medium-price hotel and you've got medium-price clothes and a whole middle-class feeling to you. You aren't the idle rich. And you're too mad at everybody to be con artists. Besides, you paid me. You're checked into the hotel by the week, for the cheaper rate. You figure to be here longer than a little, but not long enough to sign a lease on an apartment or get a job or anything like that."

He swallowed coffee again. When the spoon stuck into his cheek, it made him look wolfish. Otherwise, he looked soft.

"You're not salesmen or anything like that," he said. "I've been in your hotel room twice, and there's not a thing there to say somebody's employed you. There would be. Display case, envelope from the main office, something. You go out late in the morning, you spend all day away. At night, you drink quietly in the room. One of you hires me to check a license plate, and the other one gets mad. Doesn't want his business told around. The license plate turns out to be stolen. I'm told to go away."

"Why didn't you?" I asked him.

He shrugged. "I told you. A ratty office in a ratty neighborhood downtown. It depressed me. You two puzzled me. So I looked you up." He grinned, bringing the wolf look back. "You're Willard and Raymond Kelly," he said. "Sons of a mob lawyer who pulled out of town way back when. Is it your father you're working for?"

"Not exactly. He's dead."

"Oh. Sorry."

"Not at all." I finished the toast and the last of the coffee.

He sat there chewing a thumbnail. He was stupid, but shrewd. I should have left, but I waited. Bill lit us cigarettes.

Then he stopped chewing the nail and said, "Oh." He looked at me, grinning again. "Do you tell me, or do I go look it up?"

"All right," I said. "He was shot."

"Sure. I knew you were looking for something. I couldn't figure what." He leaned forward. "All right. I'm a cheap fifth-rate investigator. I can barely scrape up the license fee every year. But I've been in this business for twelve years. I have the contacts, I know how to look and where to look. I could maybe save you time."

I said, "I have one question. Why should we trust you?"

"Because I'm fifth-rate. Poor but honest, that's me. I'd like to do a job because it's interesting."

I chewed my cheek. "There isn't anything I can think of for you to do."

His grin was sour. "You two talk it over. You probably won't find me in the office, but leave a message with the answering service. If you want me for anything, that is." He got to his feet, took his coffee check, nodded to us both, and left.

Bill said, "I trust him, Ray. I think he's all right."

"I want to trust him," I said, "but I'm not going to."

"Maybe we could use his help."

"We'll worry about that when the time comes." I lit a new cigarette. We paid our checks and went out to the sidewalk. "I tell you what," I said. "You go on down to the library and look him up in the *New York Times Index*. He said he'd been working twelve years. Maybe he made the paper once. I'd like to be able to check him out."

I told him how to get to the library, and then I went back to the room.

I was there half an hour when Krishman called. He was mad, but controlling it. "I read in this morning's paper," he said, "that Andrew McArdle was dead."

"Yes. Heart attack."

"Did you have anything to do with that? I want the truth. Were you there?"

"We were there."

"Andrew had nothing to do with your father's death."

"And I had nothing to do with Andrew's. I didn't want him dead. He knew something. He would have told me, if he'd lived."

"Knew something? About what? Don't be ridiculous."

"Somebody told my father to get out of New York. Back in 1940. McArdle knew who."

"That's nonsense."

"He said you were a fool. He said you never knew anything."

"What? That's a lie. Andrew wouldn't say such a thing."

I said, "Goodbye." I hung up.

When Bill called, he said, "Twice. Once, he was along as witness for divorce evidence. With a husband breaking in on a wife in a hotel room. Somebody'd killed the wife when they went in. Johnson was mentioned as a witness, that's all. There were a couple more stories on the murder, but nothing about him."

"Okay. Any police names?"

"Detective Winkler. Homicide West. They have two homicide offices here, did you know that? East and West."

"Winkler," I said, writing it down. "What about the other one?"

"His car was blown up. About three years ago. There was a policeman named Linkovich at the wheel. There wasn't any explanation, and I couldn't find any later stories on it at all."

"Okay, I'll call Winkler. You come on back. How long ago was this?"

"The divorce evidence thing? Four years ago. April or May, I forget which."

It took a while to get through to Winkler and then he said, "Johnson? Private detective? I'm not sure."

"There was a woman found killed in a hotel room," I said. "Four years ago. Her husband and Johnson found her. They were there to get divorce evidence."

"Yeah, wait a second," he said. "I remember that. Edward Johnson. Vaguely. What about him?"

"I'm thinking of hiring him," I said. "But I wanted to get a recommendation I could trust first."

"Did he tell you to call me?"

"No. I found your name in the *Times*. The story on that hotel killing."

"Oh. Because I barely remember the guy. Hold on a minute."

I held on. After a while, a man named Clark came on the line. "You want a recommendation on Edward Johnson, is that it?"

"That's it."

"Okay. He's honest. He's also stubborn, and a coward. He's efficient, but don't ask him to do anything dangerous because he won't."

"But he is honest."

"I think you can count on it, yes."

I thanked him. Then I looked up Robert Campbell in the Brooklyn phone directory. There were two of them. I dialed the first one and asked for Dorothea and the woman said, "This is she."

"Wrong number," I said, and hung up. Then I copied down the address: 652 East 21st Street. I got out the Brooklyn map and the street guide. I found the address, and penciled a route to it. Then Bill came back and we got the car out.

Eleven

It was a decayed genteel apartment building, with iron grillwork on the front doors and no elevator. We climbed the stairs to 4A and rang the bell.

Dorothea Campbell was about fifty, tall and stocky and gray-haired. Decayed genteel, like the building. She wore a housecoat and an apron and scuffed slippers. Her face was cold. She had the right and the power to close the door in our faces if she felt like it. She wasn't used to power, she might abuse it.

"Hello," I said. "I'm Ray Kelly. This is my brother, Bill. Our father used to be your brother's lawyer."

"My brother?" Her voice was cold, too. "What brother?"

"Eddie Kapp."

She shook her head. "I don't have any brother." The door started to close.

"We don't have any father," I said.

The door stopped midway. "What do you mean?"

"He's dead. He did wrong things when he was young. But we never turned our backs on him."

"Eddie Kapp put me through hell," she said angrily. But she was being defensive about it. I waited, and then she let go of the door and turned away. "Oh, come in if you have to," she said. "Tell me what you want."

"Thank you."

We went in, and I was the one who closed the door.

The living room was small, and the furniture was all too big for it. The colors were dull. The metal-cabinet television set looked as though it had been left in that corner by accident.

We sat down on a fat green sofa, and she sat facing us in a matching chair. I said, "Did you ever know Willard Kelly? Your brother's lawyer. People say Bill here looks a lot like he did."

"I was eight years younger than my brother," she said. "Even if we'd been the same age, we wouldn't have known the same people. I never had anything to do with his cronies at all."

"This wasn't exactly a crony. It was his lawyer."

She shook her head stubbornly. She didn't intend to think about 1940.

I shrugged. She probably didn't have a memory to

avoid, not one that was useful to me. I said, "Is Eddie out of jail yet, do you know?"

"September fifteenth."

"That's when he gets out?"

"He sent me a letter. I threw it away. I don't care what happens to him. Let him rot in prison. I don't care. I don't want his dirty money!"

"He offered you money?"

"I don't need his pity. A man twenty-two years in prison! And he has the gall to pity *me!*" She remembered she was thinking out loud, and there were strangers present. Her mouth twisted shut like a tricky knot.

"He's still in Dannemora?"

"How do I know who you are?" she demanded.

I took out my wallet and tossed it into her lap. She looked suddenly ashamed. "I don't know," she said. "Sometimes, I don't think there's any justice in the world at all. I don't know what to think any more, I don't know what to do."

"He's in Dannemora?"

"I wish he'd stay there. I wish he wouldn't write me. After twenty-two years of silence."

"And he's getting out next Thursday, is that right? The fifteenth?"

"So soon?" Desperation flickered in her eyes. "What am I going to do?"

"He wants to stay here?"

"No, he—He wants me to leave my husband. Brother and sister. He wrote that I was all the family he had. That he had plenty of money. We could live in Florida." She looked around at what Robert Campbell had given her.

"My daughter works for the phone company," she said suddenly. She looked at me again. "I didn't realize it was so soon. Next Thursday. I didn't write him back. I threw his letter away."

She looked at the window. It faced an airshaft running down through the middle of the building.

I got to my feet, walked over, took my wallet back from her lap. "Thank you," I said.

"Yes," she said, distracted. She kept looking out at the airshaft.

Bill and I walked over to the door. I opened it, and then she turned and stared at us as though she'd never seen us before. She said, "What am I going to do?"

I told her, "Don't count on Eddie."

She started to cry.

We went downstairs and walked back to the car. Bill said, "Now where?"

"Morris Silber," I said. "I didn't find any obituary on him, but there's nobody by that name in the phone book."

"Who was he?"

"The landlord Dad defended when he got the write-up in the *Times.*"

"Hell, kid, that was thirty years ago. He died in Florida long ago."

I took a cigarette out, but it broke in my fingers. I threw it out the window, and got another one. "I can't get hold of the story," I said. "It was all so goddamn long ago. People have died, changed, forgotten, reformed, moved away. Nobody cares any more. Dad had a whole file of regular clients, and most of them came from the underworld. We know two of them. Eddie Kapp and

Morris Silber. Kapp's in jail. God knows where Silber is. Nobody knows or cares who the rest of the clients were. We can't even be sure it was Eddie Kapp that Dad meant. Or what exactly he was tying to say. Eddie Kapp did it? Eddie Kapp would know who did it? Maybe he meant Eddie Kapp would be on our side. We don't know enough about anything. And nobody else knows any more, either."

"Somebody must, or they wouldn't have started killing people."

"Morris Silber," I said. "He might know a couple other clients. They might know some more. With a starting point, after a while we could probably have the whole list."

"That would take a lot of time, Ray."

"Time's the only thing I've got." I looked at him, but he didn't say anything. I said, "I know, it's different for you. You've got the job, and the kid. House and car and the whole thing. I don't have any of that."

"I'm going to have to go back pretty soon, Ray. I'm sorry."

"If only we had a starting point."

He scratched his nose and said, "What about the guy who did the profile in the *Times?*"

Every once in a while, Bill said something brilliant like that. I said, "Let's go back to Manhattan."

Twelve

His name was Arnold Beeworthy. I found him in the Queens directory, on 74th Road. He was the only Arnold Beeworthy in New York City. NEwtown 9-9970. I called from a drugstore, and a sleepy, heavy baritone answered. I said, "Did you used to work for the New York *Times?*"

"I still do. What the hell time is it?"

"A little after one."

"Oh. All right, I ought to get up anyway. Hold on a second."

I heard the click of the lighter, then he came back. "All right, what is it?"

"You once did a profile of my father, Willard Kelly."

"I did? When?"

"1931."

"Holy hell, boy, don't talk like that!"

"It wasn't you?" He didn't sound old enough.

"It was me, but you don't have to remind me."

"Oh. Can I come out and talk to you?"

"Why not? But make it this afternoon, if you can. I have to go to work at eight."

"All right."

We had lunch first, but didn't go back to the hotel. Then we went out to Queens. We started on the same route as yesterday, when we went to see McArdle. Then we turned off onto Woodhaven Boulevard.

The cross-streets were all numbered. Some of them

were avenues and some of them were roads and some of them were streets. We saw 74th Avenue. The next block was the one we wanted, 74th Road.

Beeworthy lived in a block of brick two-story houses all attached together at the sides. His was in the middle. There was a white-painted, jagged-edged board on a stick set into the middle of the narrow lawn. Reflector letters were on the board: BEEWORTHY. It looked like one name, and sounded like another.

A woman who hadn't had Eddie Kapp for a brother or Robert Campbell for a husband opened the door, smiling at us, saying we must be Kelly. Both of us? "That's right. I'm Ray and this is Bill."

"Come in. Arnie's chewing bones in his den."

It was the kind of house sea captains are supposed to retire in. Small and airy rooms, with lots of whatnots around.

We went downstairs to the cellar. It had been finished. There was a game room with knotty pine walls. To the right there was a knotty-pine door. A sign on it said, SNARL. It had been hand-lettered, with a ruler.

She knocked, and somebody inside snarled. She opened the door and said, "Two Kellys. They're here."

"More coffee," he said.

"I know." She turned to us. "How do you like your coffee?"

"Just black. Both of us."

"All right, fine."

She went upstairs, and we went into the den. Arnold Beeworthy was a big patriarch with a gray bushy mustache. Maybe he'd always looked forty. If he was writing profiles for the *Times* in 1931, he had to be nearly sixty anyway.

The den was small and square. Rubble and paraphernalia and things around the walls and on the tables. A desk to the right, old and beaten, with mismatched drawer handles. Cartoons and calendars and photographs and matchbooks and notes were thumbtacked to the wall over the desk. A filing cabinet was to the left of the desk, second drawer open. A manila folder lay open on top of all the other junk on the desk.

His swivel chair squawked. He said, "It's too early to stand. How are you?" He jabbed a thick hand at us.

After the handshake and the introductions, Bill took the kitchen chair and I found a folding chair where Beeworthy said it would be, behind the drape.

"1931 is a long time ago," said Beeworthy. He tapped the open folder. "I didn't remember the piece you meant. Had to look it up." He swiveled the chair around and smacked his palm against the side of the open file drawer. "I've got a file here," he said, "of every damn thing I've ever written. Some day it'll come in handy. I can't think how." He grinned at himself. "Maybe I'll write a book for George Braziller," he said. "It's fantastic how things that are exciting in life can be so dull in print. I wonder if the reverse is true. It's a stupid world. And what can I do for you two?" He aimed a thick finger at Bill. "Do you look like your father?"

"I guess so," said Bill. "That's what people say."

"One thing triggers another. When you called, I didn't know a Kelly from a kilowatt. Then I read that damn thing, and I remembered the look of that son of a bitch

Silber in court, and then I remembered the lawyer. Wore a blue suit. I can't remember what color tie. Anyway, I'm sorry about that piece. I was young and idealistic, then. Went with a girl, a Jewish Communist vegetarian from the Bronx. She gave speeches in bed. That was 1931, a Communist then was somebody who didn't change their shorts every day. I've never been any damn good at interviews, I always do all the talking myself." The finger shot out at me this time, and he said, "What the hell are *you* so mad about?"

I realized then how tense my face muscles were. I tried to relax them, and it felt awkward, as though I were staring.

He grinned at me. "Okay, you've got a problem. It's a little late to be mad at me for what I said about your father thirty years ago. I take it this is something more current."

I said, "Two months ago Monday, somebody murdered my father. The cops gave up. It's something from before 1940. We need names."

He sat still for a few seconds, looking at me, and then he got to his feet and took one step to his right. "I want to record this. Do you mind?"

"Yes."

He looked back at me. One hand was on the tape control. "Why?"

"We don't want anything in the paper. They're after us, too. The whole family. They killed his wife already, three weeks ago."

Bill said, "Two weeks and three days."

"All right, this is off the record. Nothing in the paper

unless you say so. Unless and until." He stepped back, pulled open a green metal locker door, pointed at the shelf. Red and black tape boxes. "I save that crap, too," he said. "Interviews that go back nine years. Useless. Not a celebrity in the crowd."

There was a knock at the door. He snarled, and his wife called, "Open up, my hands are full."

Bill jumped up and opened the door.

She had a round tray that said Ruppert's Knicker-bocker Beer on it. She set the three cups of coffee around on spaces we cleared. She smiled at everybody, but didn't say anything, and went right out again, closing the door after her. Beeworthy said, "Will you take my word for it?"

I wanted his cooperation. He was a complicated string-saver. I said, "All right."

"Fine." He clicked it on, and the tape reels started slowly turning. He went back to the desk and sat down and pushed papers out of the way, and there was the microphone.

Then he had me tell the story, in detail. I didn't like spending the time, but I was the one asking the favor.

He was a fake. He knew how to interview. Three or four times he asked questions, and filled in sections I'd blurred. He said, "You're grabbing for the wrong end of the horse. Find out who's around *now*, and then see which of them knew your father when. I could do that probably easier than you. Some of Eddie Kapp's old cronies, maybe. Let me dig around in the files—not here, at the paper—and I'll give you a call on Monday. Where you staying?"

"I don't think there'll ever be any story in this," I said. "Not that I'd want you to print."

He laughed and tugged at his mustache. "Don't believe the reporters you see in the movies," he said. "The age of creative journalism is dead. Stories today are things editors point at. I want this for me, strictly for my own distraction and edification." He got up and switched off the tape recorder. "What I really ought to be doing," he said, looking at the tape reels, "I ought to be editing some small-town paper somewhere. Up in New England somewhere. I never made the move. I should have made the goddamn move." He turned back. "I'll look things up," he said. "Where can I get in touch with you?"

"Amington Hotel."

"I'll call you Monday."

He went upstairs with us. His wife showed up long enough to say goodbye. She smiled and said, "I hope you didn't sell him a treasure map. I don't think I could take another treasure map."

Bill grinned. "No treasure map," he said.

Beeworthy handed her his cup. "Coffee," he said.

He stood in the doorway as we went down the walk to the car. He looked too big for the house. He said, "I'll call you Monday."

Thirteen

Bill twisted the car around side streets back to Woodhaven Boulevard. "Where to?"

"Manhattan," I said.

"Okay." He made a right turn. "Any place special?"

"Lafayette Street. Johnson's office."

"You trust him now?"

"Part of the way. I don't think he'd lie to us. He seems to have the idea he could help. I want to know how."

"What street was that? You better look it up."

I opened the glove compartment and got out the map and street guide. It wasn't that tough to find. But the nearest parking space was four blocks away. We walked back and took the elevator to the fifth floor. It was a run-down building with green halls. Johnson's office was 508, to the right.

It was one room. Desk, filing cabinet, wastebasket, two chairs, all bought secondhand. Walls the same green as the hall. One window, with a view of a tarred bumpy roof and beyond it a brick building side. The ceiling paint was flaking.

Johnson stood in the corner, wedged between a wall-turn and the filing cabinet. His one arm was up resting on top of the cabinet. His face was bloody. He looked as though he'd been standing there a long time.

He turned his head slowly when we came in. "Hello," he said. His voice was low and flat, his pronunciation bad.

His lips were puffed. "I was going to call you," he said carefully.

We went over and took his arms and led him over to his desk. We sat him down and I said, "Where's the head?"

"Left."

I went down the hall to the left and found it. The tile floor was filthy. I got a lot of paper towels, some wet and some dry, and went back.

Bill had a bottle and glass out of a drawer. He was pouring into the glass. I said, "Let me wash the face first."

He grunted when I touched the towels to his face. Wet first, and then dry. Somebody'd been wearing a ring. He had scrapes on both cheeks and around his mouth. Bill handed him the glass and he said, "Thanks."

I wet a couple of towels from the bottle. When he put the glass down, I said, "Hold still."

He tried to jump away when I pressed the towels to the scrapes, but I held his head. "Christ sake!" he shouted. "Christ sake!"

I finished and stepped back. "Okay, have another snort."

He did, and Bill handed him a lit cigarette. His hands were shaking.

I said, "How long ago?"

"Half an hour? Fifteen minutes? I don't know. I just stood there."

"Why were you going to call us?"

He motioned vaguely at his face. "This was because of you. They wanted to know where you were."

"And you told them."

He looked down at his hands. "Not at first."

"It's all right. We've been looking for them, too. You did right telling them."

He emptied the glass and reached for the bottle. He drank from the bottle.

I said, "Where did they connect you with us? They didn't see us together, or they'd know where to find us. You've mentioned our names to somebody."

He coughed and dragged on the cigarette. "Half a dozen people. A couple cops I know, a reporter, a guy works for one of the big agencies."

"It's one of them. You find out which one. You need any money?"

"Not now. Later on, maybe. Unless you could advance me twenty."

I nodded at Bill. He dragged out his wallet and gave Johnson two tens.

I said, "Move as quick as you can. And don't be afraid to talk. If they come after you again, tell them anything they want to know. It's okay."

"Yeah."

"Call us at the hotel as soon as you've got something. If we're not there, leave a message."

"You aren't going to move?"

"Why should we? I told you, we want to find them as bad as they want to find us. We'll stay at the same place."

He shook his head. "They're mean bastards," he said.

"You okay now?"

"Yeah, I guess."

We left and went uptown and checked into a hotel

forty blocks north of the Amington. We hung around, and when I called the Amington they said there weren't any messages.

We bought a deck of cards and hung around the room. All we could do was wait.

Fourteen

Bill woke me up at nine o'clock in the morning and said it was time to go to Mass. He wasn't kidding. I said, "No."

"You need God's help, Ray," he said earnestly.

I said, "Go away."

"You don't think you do?"

"The guys in the Chrysler didn't."

"Who?"

"The guys who killed Dad. And your wife."

"Ray, you're still in the Church, aren't you?"

"Do I look it?"

"You've lost your faith?"

"They shot it out from under me."

"You're one of those, huh? The first tragedy comes into your life, and you blame it on God."

I rolled over on my side away from him. "Go on," I said. "You'll be late for Mass."

He did some more talking, but I ignored him, so he got dressed and went out. I fell asleep again.

I was awake when he came back. I was sitting by the window, looking out at the street and thinking about waking up in the hospital.

He put a bag on the dresser. "I brought you coffee and a danish," he said.

"Thanks."

He had the same for himself. We were quiet and ate for a while, and then we both started to apologize at the same time. We broke off and laughed, shaking our heads. "Yeah," I said. "I was tired, that's all."

"I should of left you alone."

"The hell. I don't like this waiting."

He grinned and shrugged. "We need to wait, that's all. We've gone this far, now we wait." His hand was wrapped around the coffee carton. He tilted it, finishing the coffee, and then tossed it into the can. "All we have to do is take it easy."

"Yeah."

I went over and called the other hotel and asked if there were any messages. There weren't. I went back, and Bill had a rummy hand dealt out on his bed. I scooped up my cards and played standing up, walking around between draws. I went gin on his seventh discard and picked up forty-three points and threw the cards down on the bed and lit a cigarette. Bill told me to take it easy. I walked around some more, and then I came back and shuffled the cards and dealt out the second hand. By the time I went gin I was sitting down.

At quarter to three, I went down and signed for another day and paid. Then I went back up and picked up the hand Bill dealt me and ripped the cards across the middle, so we went out and had hamburgers and bottles of Schlitz. Bill said, "I think we can go back and get the suitcases now. What do you think?"

I shrugged. "What the hell. Anything."

We got the car. Bill drove and I sat beside him and chain-smoked. I looked out at the people. Two months ago less one day I was here with Dad. One of those people out there recognized Dad and went and made a phone call. Or shadowed us back to the hotel first. One of those people on the sidewalk. I wanted to know which one. I wanted to reach out of the car and grab him by the throat, and drag him along beside the door.

We stuck the car in a parking lot and walked uptown and crosstown and came at our hotel from the back, where there was a dry-cleaning store. A little store in the back corner of the hotel, on the side street, open on Sunday for the tourists.

We went in. There was a good-looking colored girl in a green dress behind the counter. I said, "Hotel maintenance. Survey check. We got to get into the cellar here."

She shrugged. "Okay with me."

I looked around and acted mad. "Lady, I'm not playing guessing games with you. I don't have the whole damn hotel memorized. Where's the door?"

She waved a hand. "Back there. You'll have to move that rack."

We went behind the counter, down between the racks of cleaned clothes, and I saw the lines of the door in the linoleum floor. I shoved the rack out of the way, and the girl said, "Take it easy with the clothes."

I ignored her. I lifted the door, and it was pitch-black down there. We didn't have any flashlight, and it wouldn't have looked good to back out. I just hoped there was a light switch somewhere.

I just barely saw it as I was going down, tucked away behind a beam next to the door opening. I clicked it on, and continued down, and Bill came after me.

There was a wide, balanced firedoor off to the right. It was filthy dirty. Instead of a lock, there was a latch and hasp, held shut by a twisted piece of thick wire broken off a hanger. By the time I got it untwisted, my hands were coated with dirt. My forehead was wet with perspiration, and I could almost feel the dust settling against it and sticking.

I shoved the door aside on its roller and pawed around on the other side till I found the switch. I turned it on and saw a bigger chunk of basement, just as filthy as this. Up ahead, there was humming. Machinery, not voice.

I went back to the foot of the stairs and shouted up. The girl came over and looked down at me. She stood with her legs pressed together and her palms flat against the front of her thighs, so I couldn't peek up under her skirt. She said, "I got a customer here. What do you want?"

"We're going on through this way," I said. "You can close that door now."

She started to bitch about it. I turned away and went through to the other part of the cellar. Bill was already over there, waiting for me. The girl kept bitching about how it wasn't her job to close trap doors. I pulled the firedoor shut and then I couldn't hear her.

Off this room there was a corridor, low-ceilinged, with concrete walls. The walls were dirt-gray except where fresh concrete had dribbled away and showed flaky white. At the end there was another firedoor. This one wasn't fastened at all. We slid it open and went through to a part that was already lit. The humming was louder ahead of us.

We came to the end of the corridor a little ways after that door, and found a relatively clean part, with an old chunk of linoleum on the floor, and a battered old desk, and a girlie calendar on the wall. There wasn't anybody there except a cat asleep beside the desk. The cat woke up when we got there, and slunk away to the doorway where the humming came from. It was brightly lit in there. I got a glimpse of metal stairs going down and a lot of dirty black machinery and a guy with a white house-painter's cap sitting on a kitchen chair.

On the opposite wall, there was the door of the freight elevator. I pushed the button, and you could hear the loud groaning of the machinery in the bottom of the elevator shaft, even farther down than we were. The elevator came. It wasn't fancy, like the one for the customers. It had wide plank flooring and chest-high sides and only a kind of grillwork on top and a grill gate at the front. We got on and I shut the gate and pressed the button for our floor. The elevator ground up slowly and stopped, and we got off. I pressed the top button and unlocked and closed the door. It went on up.

We came down the hall from the opposite direction that we usually took. There was nobody around. There was a telephone ringing. When we got closer, I could hear it was coming from our room. It rang six times and quit.

I listened at the door of the room. Then I unlocked it and shoved it open fast and ran in crouched, cutting to the right while Bill faded to the left. But I'd heard right, there wasn't anybody there.

We packed what we needed in one bag and left the other one still open on a chair. Then we rumpled the beds. The place had been searched. Quietly, with things put back more or less in the right spot. Nothing had been taken, not even the two guns.

We went out to the hall, and I was just putting the key in the lock when the phone started again. Bill said to forget it but I told him, "No, we still live here. We don't want them looking somewhere else."

I went back in and picked it up on the fifth ring. A guy's voice said, "Kelly?"

"That's me," I said. Behind me, Bill brought the suitcase back in and shut the door.

"Will Kelly? Will Kelly, Junior?"

"No, this is Ray."

"Let me talk to Will."

"Who shall I tell him is calling?"

"Never you mind, kid brother. You just put Will on, okay?"

"Yeah, sure. Hold on. I'll get my big brudda for ya."

"Thanks." He thought he was the one being sarcastic.

I dropped the phone on the table and said to Bill, "Some guy. He'll only talk to you. But he says Will instead of Bill."

"Okay." He came over and reached for the phone. When his fingers touched it, I saw the stagefright hit him, and I said, "What the hell. All you have to do is listen."

"Yeah." He picked it up and held it to his face and said, "Bill Kelly here." He waited and said, "Why?" Then he waited and said, "What's your name, friend?" Then he waited some more and said, "The hell with you." His eyes swiveled to me and he grimaced. Into the receiver he said, "No I'm not hanging up." He made writing motions with his other hand.

I went over and got the hotel's pen and a piece of the hotel's stationery. Behind me, Bill said, "For all I know, this is some sort of gag."

I came back and put the pen and paper on the table and he said, "What was that name? No, I didn't hear it." His eyes found me again and he grinned and asked the phone, "Eddie Kapp? Who the hell is Eddie Kapp?"

I grinned back at him. I lit two cigarettes and held one of them for him. I walked around the room.

"To you maybe it's comedy," Bill told the guy, "but to me I've got better things to do. You want to give me a number, go ahead."

I walked back and stood watching.

"I've got pencil and paper," Bill said. He was enjoying himself now, acting like he was bored and irritated, all his stagefright gone. He picked up the pen. "Go ahead," he said. "Shoot." He winked at me, and I nodded and laughed.

"Circle," he said, writing it down, "five, nine, nine, seven, oh. Yeah, I've got it." He read it off again. "Maybe I'll call it, maybe I won't" he said. He grinned. "Up y—" Then he looked at me. "He hung up."

"You, too. Here's a cigarette."

He traded the receiver for the cigarette. "He wouldn't give me his name. He said all he wanted was to give me the phone number. We should stick close to the room until Friday, and then we should call that number. When I asked him why, he said maybe the name Eddie Kapp would tell me."

"He's getting out Thursday," I said.

"I know."

"Hold on a second." I dialed the number, and after two rings a recorded female voice told me it wasn't a working number. I hung up. "Okay, let's get out of here. That guy's already calling his buddies in the lobby. The Kellys are home."

We went out and down the hall to the freight elevator. I'd unlocked the door on the way in. I pushed the button, and when it came down we got aboard and I pushed the lock button on the inside of the door. Then I closed the gate and we went down to the cellar.

The cat was sleeping on top of the desk. She raised her head and looked at us. Way down to our right were some whiskey cases. We went down there, and looked around. In a shallow concrete pit there were four tapped beer kegs, the copper coils running up the side wall. So it was all right, it was the bar and not the liquor store. We went over to the stairs and up them. This was a regular door, not a trap like in the cleaners. I opened it and peeked out. I was looking at the corridor between the bar and the kitchen. It was empty. We went through and made a sharp left into the men's room. We washed our faces and hands, and then went down the long length of the bar and out the street door. We turned the corner and walked crosstown and downtown to the West 46th Street parking lot where we'd left the car. There was a sullen veteran in khakis and fatigue cap on duty, and he walked back to the car with us and stood looking in through the windshield at the steering wheel as he said, "I'm taking a chance on this, but what the hell. I don't do their goddamn dirty work or anybody's."

He sneaked a quick look at us and glared back at the steering wheel again. "They screwed me out of two hundred fifty bucks. What am I going to do, call the goddamn cops on them? They got the goddamn cops in their pocket. *You* know that."

I said, "What's the point?"

His cheek twitched, and he kept staring through the windshield into the car. "I just want you to know, that's all. How come I'll do this. I'm paying the bastards back, that's what, two hundred and fifty bucks worth." He tugged at his fatigue cap, and turned around quick to look out at the street. Then he turned back. "A guy came around yesterday afternoon," he told the car, "with a sheet of paper and your license plate on it. He give me, and said I should call in at Alex's if the car shows up. He described the car, red and cream Merc like this one. Only, I wouldn't give them the sweat off my stones. And you've got an out-of-town plate, I figure you're tourists or something and they're trying to give you a bad time. So the hell with them. I didn't call. And I smeared mud on your plates."

"You did?" I went over and looked at the back of the car. He'd done a good job, realistic, with mud and dirt on the bumper and over the license plate, so a part of each number was showing. Enough so it didn't look like a covered plate, but it wasn't easy to read the numbers.

I went back and said, "Thanks. You did a good job."

"You better go back upstate," he said.

I dug out my wallet and found a ten. I slid it down the fender to him. "Here's an installment on the two-fifty," I said.

"You didn't have to, but it's okay." He palmed the ten.

"This guy, what's his name?"

"I don't know. I've heard him called Sal. Or Sol, I don't know which. He comes around sometimes, and sometimes he works here. Every once in a while, he parks some fancy car here. The boss knows him. He's big, with a great big jaw like Mussolini."

"And Alex's?"

"That's a car rental place, up by the bridge. Up in Washington Heights." He swiped another quick look at me. "You don't want to spoil with them, Mister. You better go back upstate."

"Thanks for the help," I said.

He shrugged. "You got to wait out by the sidewalk," he said. "I'll bring the car to you."

"Okay."

We walked back over the gravel to the sidewalk, and he drove the car out and gave it to us without a word. We went around the block and down to 39th Street and through the Lincoln Tunnel. In Jersey City, we parked the car on a street off Hudson Boulevard and took the tube back to Manhattan, switched to the subway and went uptown to the hotel. We unpacked the suitcase and showered and brushed our teeth.

Bill said, "Do you want to follow up this car rental place?"

I shook my head. "That's a Pacific campaign. Fight

your way across every useless little island you can find for five thousand miles, before you get to the big island you wanted all along. I want to stay away from the little islands. That's why we switched hotels. Thursday we get to the big island."

"Fine with me," he said.

Later on, we went to a movie. I couldn't sit still, so we went down to Brooklyn on the subway and drank a while at a neighborhood bar. He closed at four and we took the subway back. There wasn't anything to drink in the room. I lay on my back in the dark and stared at the ceiling. "Bill," I said, "I think I know why they futzed around on all those little islands."

But he was asleep already.

Fifteen

Monday afternoon I called the other hotel. Beeworthy and Johnson had both called, leaving messages for me to call them back. Since I now knew it was Eddie Kapp I was looking for, at least to begin with, there wasn't any point in calling either of them.

Bill went out for a deck of cards and was gone an hour. When he came back, he had a haircut and he said he didn't know I'd be worried. We played cards and I walked around and the room got smaller. We went out after a while and went to see a movie up in the Bronx. Then we went to a bar.

Tuesday, I called Johnson, just to have something to

do. He was frantic. He said, "Where the hell are you people? I've been going nuts. Did you move out or something?"

"Hell, no," I said. "We're still here. We aren't around the room much."

"Jesus Christ, I guess not. I've been over there half a dozen times. I was ready to think those guys got to you."

"Not a peep," I said.

"They haven't been around at all?"

"Nope."

"You son of a bitch, you've moved someplace else."

I grinned. It was fine just to be talking to somebody. "We're still registered at the Amington," I told him, "and our suitcase is still there. I mean here."

"All right, you shouldn't trust me with the address, but you don't have to lie to me."

"We're still at the Amington, Johnson," I said.

"All right, all right." He was irritated. "On that other thing," he said, "do you want to hear what I've got to say or not?"

"It's up to you."

"Oh, crap. You're just trying to get under my skin. I've got it narrowed down to two people. A cop named Fred Maine. And a guy named Dan Christie, he's an investigator works for Northeastern Agency. It's got to be one of those two. I'm pretty sure Maine gets two paychecks every week, one of them from the city. And Christie is a poker buddy of Sal Metusco, he's a numbers collector midtown on the west side."

"Keep up the good work," I told him. I didn't say anything about the veteran in the parking lot, because

Johnson would only have told the next guy who broke his arm.

We talked a little, about nothing at all, and I said I'd call him back. I didn't say when. Then I looked at Beeworthy's number, but I resisted the impulse. He'd want to do a lot of interviewing, and I wasn't in the mood.

Bill wanted to go to another movie that night, but I couldn't take it. So we sat around the room and drank and after a while I threw a gin hand out the window. A little after midnight, we went down to 42nd Street and saw an important movie that had been made from a Broadway play called *A Sound of Distant Drums*. It was about homosexuality and what a burden it was, but the hero bore the burden girlfully. It didn't convert me.

Wednesday we checked out of the hotel. We also went down and checked out of the Amington. We figured they were looking for us somewhere else by now, so we didn't sneak around. Nobody noticed us particularly. Then we took the tube to Jersey City and got the car and drove up to Plattsburg. I rode in the back seat because I still couldn't face highway driving in the right front. Sitting back there, I read the papers we'd bought in the city. The *Post* had an article about Eddie Kapp getting out of prison tomorrow. They were unhappy about it, and wanted to know if Eddie Kapp had really paid his debt to society. There was a blurred photo of him twenty-five years ago. No other paper referred to him at all.

In Plattsburg, we checked into a hotel on Margaret Street. Bill was bushed, he'd driven three hundred and thirty miles in eight hours. I went out alone and found a bar and traded war stories with a guy who'd been stationed in Japan. If he was telling the truth, he had a better time in Japan than I did in Germany. If I was telling the truth, so did I.

In the morning, we checked out again and drove the fifteen miles to Dannemora.

Dannemora is a little town. In most of it, you wouldn't know there was a penitentiary around at all. The town doesn't look dirty enough, or mean enough. But the penitentiary's there, a high long wall next to the sidewalk along the street. The sidewalk's cracked and frost-heaved over there. On the other side, it's cleaner and there's half a dozen bars with neon signs that say Budweiser and Genesee. National and local beers on tap. Bill had Budweiser and I had Genesee. It tasted like beer.

The bar was dark, but it was done in light wood lightly varnished and it was wider than it should have been for its depth. You got the feeling the bar wasn't dark at all really, you were just slowly going blind. The bartender was a short wide man with a black mustache. There were two other customers, in red-and-black hunting jackets and high leather boots. They were local citizens, and they were drinking bar scotch with Canada Dry ginger ale.

The *Post* had said Eddie Kapp would be a free man at noon, but we didn't know for sure. We got to town shortly before ten and sat on high stools in this bar where we could see the metal door in the wall across the way. I wasn't sure I'd recognize Eddie Kapp. The picture in the *Post* was blurred and twenty-five years old. But he was sixty-one years of age. And how many people would be getting out all in one day?

We sat there and nursed our beers. I wore my shirt-tail out, and when I sat leaning forward with my elbows on the bar, the butt of Smitty's gun stuck into my lowest rib. Bill had the same problem with the Luger.

At eleven-thirty a tan-and-cream Chrysler slid to the curb in front of the bar. Bill looked at it and turned to me and said, "Is that them? Is that the ones who killed Dad?"

I didn't say anything. I was looking at the guy in the right front seat. I knew him when.

I started to get down from the stool, flipping the shirt-tail out of the way, but Bill grabbed my elbow and whispered, "Don't be a jerk. Wait till Kapp comes out."

I stood there, not moving one way or the other. The gun butt felt funny in my hand. The side that had been against my skin was hot and moist. The other side was cold and dry.

Then I said, "All right. You're right." He let me go and I said, "I'll be right back." I let go of the gun and smoothed the shirt-tail and walked down the length of the bar past the other two customers, who were talking to the bartender about trout. I went into the head. There was one stall. I went in there and latched the door and took the gun out from under my belt so I could lean over. Then I threw up in the toilet. I washed my mouth out at the sink and got back to the stall just in time to throw up again. I waited a minute, and then washed my mouth out again. There was a bubbled dirty mirror over the sink and I saw myself in it. I looked pale and young and unready. The gun barrel was cold against my hairless belly. I was a son of a bitch and a bad son.

I went back out and sat down at the stool and held my

glass without drinking. Bill said, "Nothing new." I didn't answer him.

After a while, I got fantastically hungry, all of a sudden. I waited, but a little before one I asked the bartender what sandwiches he had and he said he had a machine that made hamburgers in thirty seconds. I ordered two and Bill ordered one. The machine was down at the other end of the bar, a chrome-sided infra-red cooker.

I was halfway through the second hamburger when the door across the street opened and an old man without a hat came out.

His suit, even from across the street, looked expensive and up to the minute. It hadn't been given him by the government. It was gray and flattering. His shoes were black and caught the sunlight. His hair was a very pale gray, not quite white. None of it had fallen out. His face was tough to see from this far away; squarish and thick-browed, that was about all.

As soon as he came out, I spat my mouthful of hamburger onto the plate and got off the stool. Bill said, "Wait till he reaches the car."

I said, "Yeah, sure."

I walked over by the door. Only Kapp wasn't coming toward the car, he was turning and walking in the other direction. His shadow trailed him aslant along the wall.

He had to be Eddie Kapp. Age and timing. Expensive suit.

The Chrysler slid forward, staying close to the curb. It purred down the block, moving at the same rate as Kapp, keeping behind him. He didn't look around at it. Apparently, he hadn't seen it.

Bill said, "What the hell is that all about?"

I said, "Go get the car. Stay at least a block behind me."

He shook his head, baffled. "Okay," he said, and went out to the car. The bartender and the other two customers were looking at me. I went out onto the sidewalk and strolled along after the Chrysler.

We went three blocks that way, like some stupid parade. Kapp out in front, on the left-hand side of the street. Then the Chrysler, on the right side, half a block behind him. Then me, also on the right side, another half a block back. And then Bill, a full block behind me on this side, in the Mercury. Kapp was headed for the bus depot, from the direction he was taking. Downtown, anyway.

Then we got to a quiet block, and the Chrysler jolted ahead, angling sharp across the empty street, and it was clear they meant to run him down. I shouted, "Look out!" and ran out across the street after the Chrysler. The goddamn ankle slowed me down.

Kapp turned when I shouted, saw the Chrysler jumping the curb at him, and dove backwards through a hedge onto a lawn. A dog started yapping. The Chrysler jounced around on a parabola back to the street, up and down the curb. The guy on the right had his head and arm out the window, and was shooting at me, the way he'd shot at Dad. He had a little mustache.

I dragged Smitty's gun out and pointed it down the street and pulled the trigger six times. The guy's head slumped down, and his arm hung down beside the door. The Chrysler made a tight hard right turn, and the guy hanging out the window flapped the way live people don't.

I stood in the middle of the street and grinned. When I was four days in Germany, two guys took me to a Kaiserslautern whorehouse in Amiland, and I was afraid to admit I was virgin and afraid I'd be too afraid to do anything about it. The whore had been so damn indifferent I'd got mad and jumped her trying to attract her attention. I did, and she had an orgasm. She hadn't with the other two. Going back to the base, I broke a bus window for the hell of it. I felt the same way now, standing in the middle of the street and grinning, while the Chrysler took a lump of clay around the corner and out of sight.

The Mercury pulled up beside me, and Kapp came struggling back through the hedge. I could hear the dog going nuts. Kapp looked shaky and wobbly. He'd made a great dive for sixty-one, but now he was acting his age. His left trouser leg was ripped at the knee.

I stopped grinning and opened the back door of the Mercury. I threw the empty gun in there and went over and took Kapp's arm and brought him to the Mercury and shoved him inside. He acted dazed, and didn't fight back or ask questions. I got in after him, and slammed the door. A black-haired woman in a flowered apron came to a break in the hedge and looked at us. Bill tromped the accelerator and we rode away from Dannemora.

Sixteen

Kapp recovered pretty fast. He pulled Smitty's gun out
from under him and looked at it, and then turned to me.
"That was lousy shooting. It took you four shots to find
him and then you threw two bullets away."

"I've only got one eye," I said. "I have trouble with distance judgment."

"Oh. In that case, it was all right." He looked at the
back of Bill's thick neck. "If this is a heist," he said, "you
two are crazy. Nobody wants me back money bad."

"We just want to ask you one or two questions," I said.

He looked at me again, and grinned. He had white
false teeth. They looked better on him than the ones
Krishman had worn. "Were you alive when I went in
there, boy?" he asked me.

"Yes."

"Then you're just lucky you've lived this long." He hefted
the gun, holding it by the barrel. "What if I were to break
your head in with this? What's your partner going to do?"

I looked into his grin and said, "We're not playing."

He studied me a while, and then he looked sad and
dropped the gun onto the floor between our feet. "I'm an
old man," he said. "I'm ready to retire." He sat back,
showing me his profile, gazing up at the ceiling and
trying to look sick. "That hard violent world," he said,
"that's all behind me now."

"Not all," I said.

He quit joking. He turned to me and he kept his lips flat and his voice flat. "Ask your questions," he said, "and go to hell."

I said, "Why was Willard Kelly killed?"

He looked surprised, worried, wary, blank, one right after the other. He said, "Who the hell is Willard Kelly?"

I reached down and picked the gun up and tapped the butt against his knee. "I hear old men's bones are brittle," I said.

"Naw. I've got a geriatric formula. I take a spoonful of chancre pus twice a day. It's a new thing on the market for senior citizens."

"They let you read magazines. That's fine, but I'm not playing. How's your kneecap?" I tapped him again with the gun-butt, and he didn't manage to hide the wince. I said, "Why was Willard Kelly killed?"

"He had B.O."

I tapped him again. He put his hand down over his knee. His hand was older than his face; it had blue veins ropy against the skin. I tapped the back of his hand, and he said "Uh," and took the hand away and held it tight against his chest. I tapped his knee. He said, "Go on and break it, you clumsy bastard. I could use a good faint around now."

"You won't faint." I tapped him again. His face was paler, and there were strain lines around his eyes and mouth. I said, "Why was Willard Kelly killed?"

He turned his head away and glared out the window. I tapped him again.

He didn't faint. Bill bypassed Plattsburg. A few miles south he took a turnoff that promised cabins by the lake.

Lake Champlain. Another sign said, "Closed after Labor Day." It was after Labor Day.

There were white cabins with red trim, somewhat faded, fronted by a strip of blacktop. There was no one there, but previous poachers had left their rubber spoor on the blacktop.

Kapp didn't want to get out of the car. Bill came around and pulled him out by the hair and shoved him down between the cabins. He favored the left leg. We stood him up against the white clapboard back wall of a cabin. Trees screened us from the lake. Bill looked at Kapp and then at me and told me, "Remember McArdle."

"I will," I said. "I'll be careful."

Kapp said, "McArdle?"

"Andrew McArdle," I said. "I asked him some questions, but he had a bad heart and died before he could answer them. Bill was telling me to be more careful with you."

He shook his head. "I don't get it."

We stood and waited for him to think. He stood slanted against the wall holding his injured hand. The expensive suit looked bad. He was having trouble with the left leg, and the back of his left hand was swelling and turning gray. He had more lines on his face. He was tired and worried and futile. He was being brave when it didn't matter, and he knew it didn't matter, but he didn't know how to stop.

He tried to talk, and he had to take time out to clear phlegm out of his throat and spit it carefully away from us. Then he said, "I can't figure you two. Those other guys, I know who they were. I can guess, I mean. But not you two. Amateurs, asking the wrong questions…" He shook his head. "Where'd you get so mean?"

"What's a right question?" I asked him.

He looked up through branches at the sky. "I was a free man again a little while," he said.

I said, "Bill, if he doesn't open his mouth right now I'm going to kill him and to hell with it. We'll go back to the city and go by way of the little islands."

Bill frowned. "I don't like it, Ray," he said. "I don't want to have anything to do with it."

I said, "Here, take this gun up to the car and reload it. Better give me the Luger for while you're gone."

All of a sudden, Kapp laughed. He laughed like a man who's just heard a good joke at a clambake. We looked at him, and he pointed at Bill and cried, "You silly bastard, you're Will Kelly! You're Junior, you're his son!"

We just looked at him. He pushed himself out from the wall and limped toward us, grinning. "Why the hell didn't you say you were Will's goddamn kid? I couldn't place you, I couldn't figure you anywhere at all."

I said, "Stop. Hold up the reunion a second. There's still the question."

He looked at me, and his grin calmed down. "All right," he said. This time, he acted like he was at the clambake and it was his turn to tell a joke and he had a whopper saved up. "I didn't know Will'd been killed," he said. "But I know why. It was because he was holding something for me. Until I got out of jail. He was supposed to hold it and stay out of the city until I was sprung. He was killed because he was holding it and because I was going to be getting out."

"What was it he was holding?"

He nodded. "You."

"What about me?"

"You look more like your mother than your father," he said.

Then I got it. "You're a lying son of a bitch," I said.

"You look a lot more like her. I know. I see your father in the mirror every morning."

I laughed at him. "You're crazy, or you think we are. Or are you just wisecracking again?"

"It's true," he said.

Bill said, "What the hell's going on?"

I said to Kapp, "He didn't get it yet. When he does, he'll take you apart. You better say fast you were lying."

"I wasn't lying."

"It was the wrong ploy," I insisted. "Bill has a big thing about honor."

Kapp said, "We ought to sit down over a bottle of imported and talk. We've got a lot to fill in, the both of us."

Bill said, "Goddamn it, for the last time, what's going on?"

"Kapp says we're half-brothers. We shared a mother, only Willard Kelly wasn't my father."

Bill's eyebrows came down. "Who does he say is your father?"

"If he's smart, he'll change his story."

"I say it's me," said Kapp, "and it's true." He was mad at us.

Bill raised his shoulders and took a step and I tripped him. I said to Kapp, "He's going to kill you now, I swear to God he is. And there isn't a thing I can do about it."

Bill was struggling to his feet, and Kapp backed away to the wall, talking fast, mad and scared both. "Your mother was a two-bit whore out of Staten Island, a goddamn rabbit. She sucked Will Kelly into marrying her, with the first kid. The second was mine. I know it, because she was at my cabin on Lake George for six months and she only went back to Kelly because I told her to."

Bill was on his feet and I was hanging on his arm. Kapp spat words at us like darts. "Edith got exiled to a burg upstate with Will Kelly and orders to behave and never come back to the city. She couldn't stand it. She was there a year and she stuck razor blades in her wrists."

Bill threw me away, and I bounced off a tree-trunk. I shouted, "Tell him you're lying, or you're a dead man!"

Kapp flamed at me. His eyes were on fire. "And you'll have another dead father to revenge, brat!"

Bill swung a fist like knotted wood. Kapp tried to lean inside it, but he was too slow. It caught him behind the ear and dropped him on his face in the weeds. Bill bent over, reaching to pick him up again.

I came up and clubbed Bill with the Luger. He went down on his knees. Kapp crawled away downslope, and Bill fell on his legs. I rolled him over, freeing Kapp's legs, and Kapp crawled up a tree trunk to a standing position and stood hangdog, his arms around the thick trunk.

I stood in front of him, holding the Luger by the barrel. "Don't stop talking," I said.

"Not now, boy, I'm an old man."

"Stop playing!"

He shivered, and leaned his forehead against the bark. His eyes were closed. "All right," he said. "But give me a few seconds. Please."

I gave him the seconds. When he raised his head, there were fine lines from the bark on his brow. He pushed his lips over in a weak smile. "You've got her looks, boy, but you've got my guts. I'm glad of that." I didn't say anything. He shrugged and let the smile fade out, and said, "All right. Her name was Edith Stanton. She came out of Rosebank on Staten Island in '34. She went with Tom Gilley a while. He made her pregnant, but he aborted her with some right hands to the stomach. Then she floated around, here and there, with one or another of a bunch that mainly knew each other. This was still just after Repeal, and we were all trying to get organized again. She came across Will Kelly, and he fell for her. He was the only one'd ever held a door for her since Staten Island, and she liked it. Then she got pregnant again, by him this time, and suckered him into marriage. But she didn't like staying home with the kid all the time, and she got to hanging around with the old bunch. Kelly stayed home and changed diapers. I think he's waking up."

I turned and looked. "We've still got a few minutes," I said.

"All right. It's like this, some women come to life with motherhood. I never paid much attention to Edith at all before, but when she started hanging around again she was different. No, she *looked* different. Tougher, maybe. More basic. I don't know what it is, it happens to some women. I took her home. She was a rabbit, but there was something interesting in her besides that. I don't know how to explain it." He was getting nostalgic.

"I don't even care," I told him. "Get on with it."

That brought him back. He said, "For a while, in '38, there was some trouble. Baltimore was where heroin and that came into the country. There was a kind of dispute, Chicago and us, as to who was going to run Baltimore. So I went up to a private place on Lake George. I had two boys with me, two I could trust. And Edith. I told her come along and she came. We were there six months, and nobody touched her but me. She came back pregnant. She named the kid Raymond Peter Kelly. That was a private joke between her and me. I owned the cabin as Raymond Peterson."

Bill moaned. I said to Kapp, "We'll finish the conversation in the car. Come on."

"All right."

He took a step away from the tree and fell down. He looked up at me, shame etched on his face. "There was a time a workout like this would've meant nothing," he said. "Not a thing. Not a thing at all."

"I believe you."

I switched the Luger to the other hand and helped him up. He leaned on me and we went back up between the cabins and around to the Mercury. I looked at him. He wouldn't be running anywhere. I said, "I'll be right back. You won't have to go over this part again."

He nodded. I opened the back door and he sagged onto the seat, his feet hanging out onto the blacktop, his head leaning sideways against the seatback. I turned away from him and went back and found Bill coming up, one arm straight out beside him holding the cabin. His face was square gray stone.

I stood in front of him. I said, "Bill, I want you to know something."

He said, "Get out of the way."

"There's an old man up at the car. If you kill him for telling the truth, I'll shoot you down for a mad dog. What did you do when they told you Ann was dead? Punch the guy who brought the news?"

He said, "Go to hell."

I stepped aside. "You can't stamp out facts with fists," I said. "Your father was a crook's shyster. My father is sitting in the car up there. Our mother wasn't the kind they have in the *Ladies Home Journal*."

He let go the cabin and went down on his knees and started to cry with his hands hanging straight down at his sides. I went back to the Mercury and said to Kapp, "He'll be along pretty soon. He won't do anything any more."

"Good." He nodded. His eyes were half-closed, his hands were limp in his lap. The swollen hand looked worse. "I'm tired," he said. He pushed his eyelids open more and studied me. He smiled. "You're my only child, do you know that? The only child I ever fathered. I'm glad to look at you."

I lit us cigarettes.

Seventeen

September is a good time of year way upstate. I stood beside the car and smoked and looked around. The cigarette smoke was thin and blue in the air. The mountains over us in the west were half in the green of summer and half in the browns and reds of fall. The lake, seen down past the cabins and the tree trunks, was blue and deep and cold. I could smell it. Far away over it was Vermont, dark green.

I didn't look at Kapp. I didn't know how to fix my face to look at him. It wasn't as though I'd been an orphan all my life. I already had a father. Kapp had blood claims, but he was a stranger.

After a while, Bill came up into sight from between the cabins. He stood there, not looking our way, and got a cigarette for himself. He fumbled badly with it, as though his fingers had swollen. Then he came over, slow and heavy, and got silently behind the wheel and started the engine.

I didn't know who to sit beside. The front seat still made me geechy, but I didn't want Bill to think he was being cut out. Kapp knew it, and grinned at me. "Sit up front with your brother. I want to stretch out, I'm tired."

I got in and slammed the door. Bill gazed out the windshield and mumbled, "Back to the hotel?"

I said, "Might as well."

We drove back to Plattsburg. Kapp said he wanted a

drink. Bill went upstairs, walking away with his shoulders hunched, and Kapp and I went across the lobby and into the bar. It was called the Fife & Drum. The glasses were painted red, white and blue to look like drums. Because of the Revolutionary War.

Kapp said, "I haven't had a drink in fifteen years. What's a good Scotch?"

I shrugged. "I don't buy good Scotch."

The waiter stooped and murmured, "House of Lords?"

"Good name," said Kapp. "Got a ring to it. Two doubles, on the rocks."

The waiter went away. I said, "You were in jail more than twenty years. They let you have liquor the first five?"

He winked. "I should of gone to Sing Sing, boy, but I had connections. And there was a time when Dannemora was a little easier. Not like a Federal pen." He made a sour face. "It is now."

The waiter came back, went away.

Kapp raised the glass, tasted it, made a face. He coughed. "I forgot. It's like starting new, it's been so long. Remember how lousy it tasted the first time?"

"You want a mix?"

"A what? Oh, a set-up? Not me, boy. Not Eddie Kapp." He got out a new cigarette, working one-handed. His left hand looked terrible. I held out my zippo and said, "I'm sorry what I did to you."

"Shut your face. Tell me about Kelly. Your brother. He doesn't look like the type to be here."

"They killed his wife, too."

"Hah? His wife?" He sat back and nodded at me and grinned. "That means they're scared," he said. "Scared of old Eddie Kapp. That's good."

"We found a guy said there was some kind of syndicate trouble brewing in New York. That that was why they killed my—my father. Why they killed Kelly."

"Take it easy. You think of him as your father, call him your father. He was a lot more your father than I was, huh?"

"You were in jail."

"That's the truth." He swallowed some more Scotch. "I'm getting used to it," he said. Then he watched himself tap ashes into the tray. "About your mother," he said. "I don't want you to get me wrong, what I said before. Edith never worked in a house, nothing like that. She wasn't ever a professional."

"Let's forget about that."

He got mad. He glared at me. "She was a good girl," he said. "She gave me a good son."

I had to grin. "Okay."

He grinned back at me. "Okay it is, boy. And I'll tell you something, they're out of their heads. They're panicky. I can look at you two and there's no question which one of you is Will Kelly's boy. No question. But there's always the chance, always the chance. They're panicky, they're afraid of the chance. They'll even go for the kid, you wait and see."

"Do you think so?"

"You wait and see. Hah!" He sat back again, smoking like a financier, his eyes gleaming in the dim light of the bar. "We'll give them merry hell, boy! Who wants Florida?"

"The Seminoles."

"They can have it." He leaned forward fast. "You know what I was going to do? I figured I was an old man, washed-up, ready to retire. I wrote my sister—frigid-faced bitch, but I didn't know anybody else in the world—I told her leave that bum she's married to. We'll live in Florida, I've still got plenty stashed away, with an extra twenty years' interest on it. See? Old Eddie Kapp, washed-up, retired to Florida for the sun and the cheap funeral. With my *sister*."

He ground out the cigarette. "Family, family, family, that's always the same damn thing." His voice was low and grim and intense. "With the mob, with you, with me. Always the same damn thing. I was ready to spend the rest of my life with my sister. Think of it, with my sister. I hate her, she's a hypocrite, she always was."

"I met her," I said. "She's just frustrated."

He grinned. "Careful, boy, you're talking about your aunt."

I laughed. "That's right, isn't it?"

"I tell you, I'd given up. Tony and The French and all the rest, they were writing letters to me. Come on back when they spring you, Eddie, we're ready to roll. We're just waiting on you, Eddie, and we move in. Yeah, the hell with all that. That's the way I figured it, I was an old man, time to retire. And just the one relative in all the world." He curved a grin of pain. "It's family, it does it every time. Where's the damn waiter? I'm getting the taste back."

We re-ordered and it came, and Kapp went on: "I'll tell you about family. Listen, when I saw you—who knew

111

what you were or what you wanted? Twenty-two years ago it looked easy. When this baby here is in its twenties, I'll be out again, and he'll be at my side. See? But by now, who knew? You were Kelly's kid, not mine." He drank, inhaled cigarette smoke, grinned, winked at me. "Then I saw you, boy. Raymond Peter Kelly. Keep the Kelly, who cares? I saw you, and I knew you were mine." He got to his feet, looking around. "Where's the crapper?"

He had to ask a waiter. I sat and thought about him. I thought, *He copulated with a married woman named Edith Kelly and impregnated her and she produced me.* I could believe and understand that. I thought, *He is my father.* That was something else again.

He came back and sat down. He finished the second drink and we ordered thirds. They came and he went on talking as though he hadn't stopped. "This thing about family, now," he said. "It's an important thing with a lot of people. All kinds of people. And I'll tell you a group of people it's important to, and that's the people make up the mob. Particularly in New York. You don't think so? Hard cold people, you think. No. There wasn't a two-bit gun carrier on the liquor payroll didn't take his first couple grand and buy his old lady a house. Brick. It had to be brick, don't ask me why. It's in the races, national backgrounds, you know what I mean? Wops at the national level, mikes and kikes at the local level. Italians and Irish and Jews. All of them, it's family family family all the time. Am I right?"

I said, "People get assimilated. Americanized."

"Yeah, sure, I know that. Believe me, for the last few years, I did nothing but read magazines. I know all about that, when you're Americans you got no roots, you move around, all that stuff. No family homestead, no traditions, nothing. Who gives a shit about cousins, brothers, parents, anybody? Only if they're rich, huh?"

We grinned at each other. I said, "Okay. So what difference does it make?"

"I'll tell you, boy, there isn't a man in the world doesn't want to be respectable." He pointed a finger at me, and looked solemn, as though he'd spent long nights in his cell thinking about these things. "You hear me? Not a man in the world doesn't want to be respectable. As soon as a man *can* be respectable, he *is*. You got immigrants, they come into this country, how long before they're really Americanized? No roots, no traditions, who cares about family, all that stuff. How long?"

I shrugged. He wanted to answer the question himself, anyway.

"Three generations," he said. "The first generation, they don't know what's going on. They got funny accents and there's a lot of words they don't know, and they've got different ways of doing things, different things they like to eat and wear, and all the rest of it. You see? They aren't respectable. I'm not talking about honest and dishonest, I'm talking about *respect*. They're not a part of the respectable world, see? Same with their kids, they're half and half. They've got the whole upbringing in the house, with the old country stuff, and then grade school and high school and the sidewalk outside. See? Half and half. And then the third generation, Americanized. The third generation, they can be respectable. Do you see what I'm getting at?"

I said, "I don't think respectable's the word you mean."

"The hell with that." He was impatient, brushing it away. "You know what I mean. It takes three generations. And the third generation has practically no crooks in it. I mean organization crooks, the mob. That's almost all first and second generation, you see what I mean? Because every man in the world wants to be respectable, but a lot of guys are going to say, 'Okay, if I can't be respectable, I can't. But I still want to make good dough. And only the respectable types like in the *Saturday Evening Post* can get the good jobs with the good dough. But my brother-in-law drives a liquor truck bringing in the stuff from Canada and makes great dough, plus sometimes a bonus for an extra job doing this and that, so what the hell. I can't be respectable, anyway.' See what I mean?"

I nodded. "Yes, and I see what you're driving at. The first and second generations aren't Americanized. So they've got the old feeling for family."

"Right! And that's where you come in, boy." He leaned far forward over the table. "I tell you, family is *all* to these people. You kill a man, his brother kills you. Or his son. Like you, for Christ's sake, going after the guy killed Will Kelly. Or things like this, there's maybe a dispute of some kind, somebody in the mob gets killed by somebody else. And the guy who did it, or ordered it, he sends like a pension around to the other guy's wife. You know what I mean, a few bucks every week, help buy the groceries, get the kids some shoes. You know what I mean. There was a time in Chicago, '27, '28 I think it was, there was almost forty widows getting bootleg pensions all at one time. You see what I mean?"

"You said something about this being where I came in."

"Damn right." He stopped and laughed. "You know, I'm not used to all this talking, all at once like this. It makes me thirsty. And I'm not used to this Kings & Lords, whatever it is."

"House of Lords."

"Yeah. I can feel it in my head already, and what is this, my third?"

"Third, yes."

"Let's make it fourth."

We did, and he said, "The twenties, those were the years. We organized faster than the law, that was the main thing. We were one jump ahead all the time. Until this income tax thing, and I tell you that was unfair. That was a cheat. I've got no respect for the Federal Government; if you can't get a man fair, you just can't get him, you see what I mean? Now, who in the whole damn country ever filled out a tax form honest? Up till then, I mean." He shook his head. "No respect for them at all, they don't go by the rules. Anyway, the point was, we all got organized and we had thirteen good years, and then along came Repeal and we had a tough time getting readjusted, you know? Like the March of Dimes, when this Salk vaccine came along. Shot their disease right out from under them, huh? They had to go quick find some other disease. Same as us. Liquor's legal again, so there isn't the profit in it any more. So we're diversifying, there's dope and there's gambling and there's whores.

Gambling's best, it's safest. The other two, dope and whores, the people you have to deal with, by the very nature of the business they're unreliable. You see what I mean?"

I nodded, while he paused and drank.

"Of course," he said, "there's also the unions. Lepke led the way in that field, around from strikebreakers to trade associations to pocket unions. But Dewey got him, in '44. Four years after the Federals got me. Frankly, I was one of the people always thought Lepke overdid it. He gave Anastasia more work than you can imagine. Lists of fifteen, twenty people at a time. After a while, it got so that was all he was doing, making up lists of people for Anastasia's group to kill. So the unions are something else again. It's a funny thing, that's the only area with the legitimate base—you know, there's nothing illegal about unions to begin with, like there is with gambling and narcotics and whores—but it's the worst for killing and breaking things up. You know what I mean? The only area where just an innocent citizen who doesn't have anything to do with anything can get beat up or shot, because of where he works or something like that."

"What's all this got to do with me?"

He laughed, shaking his head. "I'm goddamned, boy, this House of Lords is going right up into my head. I can feel the fumes going right up into my head. The point was, I was trying to give you some of the background, you know what I mean? '33, Repeal, it all started to fall apart. Everybody's looking for a new way to make a living, fighting it out for territory and what's whose and all. And Dewey came along to make life tough. And then the

Federal Government, with this cheating income tax thing. A lot of us got moved out, one way or the other. Died or retired or went to jail or one thing and another. And these new people came in. Businessmen, you know what I mean? Respectable. No more of this blood bath stuff, that's what they wanted. Just a quiet business. Buy your protection and run your business, and let it go at that. I could see it in the papers, all through the forties, everything quieting down. Like a few years ago, the meeting at Appalachin. I could see in the papers and the magazines, everybody was surprised. Like nobody knew there was a mob any more. It called itself the Syndicate now, and people figured it wasn't real, you know what I mean? Here's a guy, he runs a bottling plant for soft drinks, and he's got sixty-five guys out to his house for a meeting, and everybody was surprised."

"That's right near Binghamton," I said. "Appalachin is. I was eighteen then. Some of us rode out in a guy's car to look at Barbara's house. Where the meeting took place."

That made him laugh again. "You see what I mean? Sightseers, for Christ's sake. People don't believe it any more. There was a time, in the thirties say, when all the people around a place like that would have stayed miles away, you never know when the shooting's going to start. Now, things've been so nice and quiet for so long, a bunch of kids go out in a car and look at the house." He shook his head. "I can't believe it. Why, there was a time, if word got around that somebody like the Genna boys, say, were in town, all the innocent citizens would have gone inside and locked the doors and crawled under the beds. The same as when Anastasia got it in '57. Nobody believed it. There he was on the floor in the barber shop with five bullets in him, and pictures in the *Daily News,* and if you say the word mobster, everybody thinks of the thirties."

"Not me," I said. "One of them shot my fa—my father."

"Just a hired gun. You'll never find him."

"Wrong. I found him today. He was the guy in the Chrysler."

"The one you hit, or the driver?"

"The one I hit."

He grinned and nodded. "Good boy. You've got a lot of Eddie Kapp in you, I swear to God."

"Yeah. We were up to '57."

"Wait." He ordered another round, took a first sip, and said, "The last few years, some of the older guys have been coming back. Back from overseas, with the heat off at last, or out of jail, or one thing and another. And these smooth new types say, 'Yeah, Pop, but we don't use shotguns any more. We use inter-office memos. Why don't you go write your memoirs for the comic books?' And what can they do? Here's organizations they set up themselves, and now they get the cold shoulder. They try something, and the lawyers and the tame cops come around. Nobody throws a bomb in the living room any more, they just nag and niggle and slip around. Typical businessmen, see what I mean? Every once in a while, there's an Albert Anastasia, he just won't get reconstructed, and the guns come out. Or like with you. But not so much any more. A good press, isn't that the phrase? Good public relations. Everything nice and quiet."

"We still haven't got to me."

"You're the ace in the hole, boy. Family, didn't I tell you? We've got all these old boys, hanging around now, waiting to move in again. But they can't move. There's nobody to set himself up for boss, that's all it takes. They've met, they've written to each other, they've talked it over. And they've decided on somebody they'll all accept to run things. Me."

He gulped down all of the drink. "I'm getting the taste back." His grin was lopsided. "I wasn't going to do it. I was going to Florida with Dot. Or without her, the hell with her. Because of you. The symbol. In 1940, I was ready to make my move. Not just New York City. Half the Atlantic Seaboard. Everything from Boston to Baltimore, the whole thing. It should have been mine years before, but I'd moved too slow. Only now I had it. I had the support. Hell, I was part of the new look myself! And then these goddamn Federal people came along with this goddamn income tax thing. And I said to some of the boys, 'When I come out, this pie is mine.' And they said, 'Eddie, you'll be sixty-four years of age. Twenty-five years is a long time.' And I said, 'They'll remember Eddie Kapp. You people will remember Eddie Kapp.' They said, 'Sure, but you're going to be an old man, Eddie. Who's going to follow you?' And I told them, 'Edith Kelly has a kid of mine. When I come out, he'll be grown. And he'll be with me.' That's what I told them." He nodded loosely, eying his empty glass. I motioned the waiter. He came and took the glass away.

Kapp watched him go. Softly, he said, "Don't you think that meant something to them? *Family*. A goddamned symbol, boy, that's what you are. A *symbol*. Eddie Kapp is bringing new blood. Eddie Kapp and his boy. That's why they want me. They got a symbol to come around, something to tie them all together."

"When my father came into New York to pick me up," I said, "somebody must have recognized him."

"Sure. For twenty-two years, who cared? Before I went in, I told Will to get out of New York and stay out, not to ever come back as long as he lived. He knew I meant it, and he did it. He didn't know why, but he didn't have to know why."

"He didn't know I was yours?"

Kapp shook his head, grinning. "He knew you weren't his. That's all he knew."

I emptied my glass. All I could see was Dad looking at me, that last second before he vomited blood. "He didn't know why they were killing him. Jesus, that's sad. Oh, good Christ, that's sad." When I waved at the waiter, my arm was stiff. I said to Kapp, "He never once let me know. I was his son. Mom was dead, he brought me up by himself. Bill and me, we were the same, exactly the same."

I couldn't talk. I waited, and when the waiter brought the glass I emptied it and told him I wanted another.

Kapp said, "They knew I was getting out soon. They saw Will Kelly in town. They got panicky. They had to get rid of Kelly, and they had to get rid of his sons. They couldn't take the chance on the symbol still meaning something." He nodded. "And it still means something," he said.

I lit a cigarette, gave it to him, lit another for myself. The waiter came with more drinks. Kapp had the cigarette in his right hand. He picked up the glass with his left hand, then grunted and dropped it, and it fell over on the table. His face looked suddenly thinner, bonier. He said, "Good God, I forgot my hand."

"Let's see it."

It was gray. A swollen oval on the back was black. I said, "The hell with this. We've got to find you a doctor."

"I didn't feel a thing," he said. "Not until I picked that glass up."

The waiter was there, looking irritated, mopping up with a red-and-white-checked cloth. I paid him, and we left, and got the name of a doctor from the desk clerk. And directions, just down the street.

We went there, and the doctor looked him over. He cut the hand, for drainage, and bandaged it up, and said it would be a couple weeks before Kapp could really use it. In the meantime, keep changing the bandage every day. And stop back in three or four days. Then he checked the left knee, because Kapp was still limping. He said that was nothing to worry about, just bruised. Kapp told him he'd walked into a chair. We both had liquor on our breath, so the doctor didn't question us.

Then we went back to the hotel and up to the room. Bill was lying on his bed. His forehead was bloody around a small hole, and he had the Luger in his right hand.

Eighteen

There were three cops I talked to. One was a local plain-clothesman, a comic relief clown who chewed cut plug. One was from the county District Attorney's office, a ferret with delusions of grandeur. And the third was State CID, an ice-gray man with no tear ducts.

I told them all about Bill's having lost his wife two months ago in an automobile accident, and his father being killed only a month before that, and how he'd been very depressed ever since, and he'd had the Luger for years but I hadn't known he'd brought it along on this trip with him. And we were just traveling around the state, basically to try to forget our recent losses. But Bill had just got steadily more and more depressed, and now he'd killed himself.

The local cop swallowed it whole, with tobacco juice. The DA's man would have liked a hotter story, but he didn't want the work of digging for it. And the CID man didn't believe a word of it, but he didn't care. He was just there to memorize my face.

So it was called suicide. To me, it looked like a lousy job of staging. Aside from the fact that Bill wouldn't have killed himself for anything. It wouldn't have occurred to him.

The local cop had called a local undertaker, who might have been his brother-in-law. He looked at me and rubbed his hands together. We both knew that he was going to cheat me down to the skin, and we both knew there wasn't a thing I could do about it.

Thursday night, I went out and got drunk. I bar-hopped out toward the air base. When I started a fight with a Staff Sergeant, the CID man came from out of the smoke and took me away. He drove a gray Ford, and he put me in it and took me back to the hotel. Before I got out, he said, "Don't do what your brother did."

I looked at him. "What did my brother do, smart man?"

"I'm not sure," he said. "Whatever it was, you take warning."

I said, "Go to hell." I fumbled the door open and lurched into the hotel. I never saw him again. Whatever had bugged him, he'd either been satisfied or had given up.

In the room, I lay in bed, and for a long while I didn't know what was wrong. Then I figured it out. I couldn't hear the sound of Bill's breathing in the next bed. I listened. He wasn't breathing anywhere in the world. Poor sweet honest Bill.

I once read a book of stories by a man named Fredric Brown. In one of them he quotes the tale of the peasant walking through the haunted wood, saying to himself, *I am a good man and have done no wrong. If devils can harm me, then there isn't any justice,* and a voice behind him says, *There isn't.*

The author didn't say so, but I know. The peasant's name was Bill.

I wished I could go talk to Kapp, but we'd decided it

would be best for us to keep away from each other until all the cops went home. It would only complicate things to bring Kapp into it. Just as I said I was alone when I found Bill.

I got up and turned on the light. I went downstairs, but all the bars in Plattsburg were closed. I went back up to the room and turned off the light and sat up in bed smoking. Every time I took a drag the room glowed red and the covers moved on the other bed. After a while I switched the light on and went to sleep.

Friday afternoon, Uncle Henry showed up from Binghamton, and we had a fight. He wanted Bill's body shipped to Binghamton, and I wanted it stuck in the ground here and now. It wasn't Bill, it was just some meat. There wasn't any Bill any more.

I won, because I was willing to pay. Then there was trouble with a priest named Warren because Bill committed suicide, so he couldn't be buried in consecrated ground. I said, "There are stupid policemen in your town, Father. Bill didn't kill himself."

He said, "I'm sorry, but the official view—"

I interrupted him, saying, "Didn't you hear about the Constitution? They separated church and state."

I said more than that, and got him mad at me. Uncle Henry was shocked, and told me so when we left: "The Church has its laws about suicide, and that's—"

"If you say that word suicide once more, I'll shove a crucifix down your throat."

"If your father were alive—" And so on.

So Saturday six hired pallbearers carried the coffin from the funeral home. There was no stop at a church for the suicide; he went straight out of town to a clipped green hill with a view of Lake Champlain, and into a hole which no priest had blessed with holy water. He would have to make do with God's rain.

Uncle Henry and I were the only ones beside the grave who had known Bill in life. The undertaker came over and wanted to know if we wanted him to say a few words. I had never known till then what a man would look like who had a complete and absolute lack of taste or sensibility. I looked at this wretch and said, "No. Not ever."

After the funeral, I arranged for storage of Bill's car. It was mine now, but I couldn't drive it till the registration had been changed, which would take too long. No one can drive a car registered to a dead man.

Uncle Henry came back to the hotel room with me. He said, "Are you coming back home with me?"

"To Binghamton? I don't have any home there."

"You do with us, if you want. Your Aunt Agatha would be happy to have you stay with us."

"I'll be right back." I went into the bathroom and sat on the floor and cried like a little kid. I wanted to be a little kid. The floor was all small hexagonal tiles. I counted them, and after a while I got up and washed my face and went back outside. Uncle Henry was standing by the window, smoking a cigar. I said, "I'm sorry. I've been in a bad mood. You were a good guy to come up here."

"It hasn't been easy for you," he said.

"I don't think I want to go back to Binghamton. Not yet."

"It's your life, Ray. But you're always welcome, you know that."

"Thank you."

We were silent a minute. He wanted to say something, and he didn't know how. I couldn't help him; I didn't know what it was he wanted to say. Finally he cleared his throat and said, "About Betsy."

"Betsy?"

"Bill's girl. We've been caring for her."

"Oh. I forgot about her."

"We'd like to keep her. I'd like to adopt her." He waited, but there wasn't anything for me to say. "Would that be all right with you?"

"Oh. Well, sure. Why ask me?"

"You're her uncle. You're her next of kin."

"I don't even know her, I've never seen her. I don't have any kind of home or anything."

"I'll start the papers then. There may be something you'll have to sign, I don't know. Where can I get in touch with you?"

"I'll write you when I get an address."

"All right."

He cleared his throat again. "I should start back. I don't like to drive at night."

I went down to the car with him. He said, "Oh, yes, one other thing. Bill's house—"

"Oh, for God's sake, not now! Some other time, some other year, let me alone!"

"Yes, all right. You're right. Be sure to send me your address. I'll take care of things till then."

He drove away, and I went to a liquor store and asked for two bottles of Old Mr. Boston before I remembered. I took them both anyway, and went back to the hotel room. I sat cross-legged on the bed and smoked and drank and thought. Very gradually, I unwound. Very gradually, I got so I could pay attention to my thoughts again.

It got slowly dark outside, and I treaded heavily through my thoughts to some conclusion I didn't yet know. And Kapp knocked on the door at a little after nine.

I got up and let him in. He said, "Your uncle gone home?"

"This afternoon," I said.

"I've been watching. You haven't had any tail. I guess they're satisfied with the suicide idea."

"Aren't you?"

"Crap. Neither are you. If that job was done by a professional, they've got a lot slacker than my day."

"I know."

He pointed a stiff finger at his forehead. "The angle was wrong," he said. "You know what I mean? Dead on that way. I saw that right away. Too high."

"Yeah, I know."

"What's that you're drinking? I brought some House of Lords." He had a brown paper bag under one arm. He took the bottle out and showed it to me. "Want some?"

"I'll stay with this."

I sat on the bed again, and he sat in the armchair in the corner. He said, "You feel like talking, Ray?"

"I think so."

"Before we found Bill dead, I was going to ask you a question. You know the question I mean."

"I suppose so."

"I want to make the move, Ray. I want to get a base

and call a few people and tell them okay, they can count on me. And the first thing they'll ask me, 'You got your son with you?' What am I going to tell them?"

I didn't say anything. I read the label on the Old Mr. Boston bottle. What I was drinking was seventy proof.

He waited, and then he spoke rapidly, as though he were trying to catch up. "I'll tell you the way it stands, Ray. This thing's going to happen, one way or another. People are coming back, people are choosing sides. If you say yes, no, it doesn't make any difference, you see what I mean? It's still going to happen." He held up a rigid finger, peered over it at me. "There's only one difference if you say no. Only the one. Eddie Kapp won't be running things. I don't know who will be—maybe there'll be a fight first, I don't know—but it won't be Eddie Kapp. I'll take my sister away from her husband and go down to Florida like I figured."

"I hear it's nice down there," I said.

He frowned. "Is that your answer?"

"I don't know. Keep talking."

"All right. I want you with me. I mean besides everything else, you know what I mean? The hell with it, you're my son. I never thought about it this way, I never knew it'd hit me this way. When I went in, you were just a—you know, just a little *thing* in a crib. I saw you maybe three four times. You weren't anybody at all yet, you know what I mean?"

"And now your heart is full."

"Okay. And my glass is empty." He refilled it from the bottle of House of Lords. "I don't expect you to feel anything like that for me," he said. "What the hell, I'm no kind of a father or anything. But it hits me, I swear to Christ it does. You're my *son*, you know what I mean?"

"Yes. I know what you mean. Forget what I said there, I didn't mean to be a smart-aleck."

"Sure, what the hell. But there's two of the reasons why I want you to stick with me, you see? Because you're my son, and it's as simple as that. And because if you're with me I can make my move. There's a lot of profit in the New York operation, Ray, take it from me. God knows how much these days."

I held up my hand. "Wait a second. Let me tell you something. That doesn't matter, it doesn't mean anything to me at all. I don't care about the New York mob. If you take it, I'm not your heir."

"If you feel that way—"

"I feel that way. Have you got any more reasons?"

"It depends what you want to do," he said.

"In what way?"

"You still want revenge? Because if you do, you should stick with me. We'll be after the same people." He drank half a glass. "It depends whether that's what you want or not," he said.

"Sure." I reached over to the nightstand and got the bottle. I didn't need the glass, so I tossed it over onto Bill's bed. I drank from the bottle, and held it, looking at it, while I talked. "I've been thinking about that," I said. "Up here, since my uncle left. Trying to figure out what I'm going to do with myself. You want to hear what I've been thinking?"

"Well, sure. Certainly. I mean, that's just exactly what I want, you see?"

"Yeah. All right, this is what I've been thinking. To

begin with, every man has to have either a home or a purpose. Do you see that? Either a place to be or something to do. Without one or the other, a man goes nuts. Or he loses his manhood, like a hobo. Or he drinks or kills himself or something else. It doesn't matter, it's just that everybody has to have one or the other."

"Okay," he said. "I can see that. Like me wanting to live with my sister. So I'd have a home if I didn't have any purpose. I can see that."

"All right. Now me, I've been a kid, that's all. So what I always had was a home. Even if I was in the Air Force in Germany, I still knew I had a home, and that was on Burbank Avenue in Binghamton, where my father lived. Then they killed him, and I didn't have any home any more. But I had a purpose instead. Vengeance. To kill my father's killer. That's enough of a purpose, isn't it?"

"Sure it is."

"Sure it is. Only then you came along. And now my father is not my father. Is revenging a foster father just as good? No, it isn't."

"What about your brother?"

"My half-brother. Wait. Let me tell it to you the way I thought it out. Right now, I'm adrift. I have neither home nor purpose, only bits and pieces of purpose. To continue the vengeance of my father-who-is-not-my-father. To revenge my sister-in-law, whom I never knew. To protect my niece, about whom I care less than nothing. To assist you in your palace revolution, in which I have no stake. To even the score for the loss of my eye, which I can never get back. To save my own life, which isn't worth saving unless I have a purpose. To avenge my half-brother, where at least my own familial blood was spilt."

"All right, what's wrong with that?"

"Avenging Bill? But I need more than that. It isn't purpose enough." I raised the bottle and lowered it. While I got out a cigarette, I said, "In all of it, there still is one purpose worth having. But it dead-ends."

He shifted in the chair. "What purpose is that?"

"Somewhere in New York City, there's a man who pointed a finger and said, 'Take away Ray Kelly's home.' Other men did it, but they were only extensions of the pointing finger. I can cut that finger off. Not because he killed a foster father or a half-brother or a half-brother's wife. But because he killed my home. He left me no choice but purpose. To kill him."

He laughed nervously, saying, "It comes around to the same thing, Ray, doesn't it?"

"To kill the man who killed the me who might have been. Not exactly the same thing, Kapp."

He emptied his glass, refilled it. "What the hell," he said, "however you say it, you're still after the same people as me. The ones running the organization in New York. Same people, different reasons. Why go off by yourself and fight them?"

"Because it's my own purpose."

"We could double up. I help you, you help me."

"Fine. What's the name of the man who owns the pointing finger?"

"What?"

"The guy who gave the order to kill Will Kelly. What's his name?"

"How the hell do I know?"

"You want the crown, Kapp. You've got to know who's wearing it now."

"Hell, yes. But you don't know this kind of organization. It might be any one of half a dozen guys. I don't know which one."

"A fair trade, Kapp. You give me the name, I'll give you two weeks. You won't need any more than that. The people you want to impress, they want to see me at first, that's all. Once you're organized, they'll be too busy to wonder where the kid is."

"You mean that? You'll stick around till we're set up?"

"Two weeks. Until—what's the date today? Thursday was the fifteenth, so this is the seventeenth. Thirty days hath September. Okay. Saturday, the first of October, I'm leaving."

"But you'll play it like you're going to be sticking around, right?"

"Sure."

"You're my son and heir, right? As far as these guys are concerned, you're set to sit in the throne when I pop off, right?"

"I'll play it that way. All you have to do is give me the name."

"I will. By the first of October, I'll know which one it was."

"Not that way, Kapp."

He jumped to his feet, slamming the empty glass on the dresser. "Goddamn it, I don't *know* which one! Ray, face it, I know it's got to be one of maybe six or seven men. I could toss out one of their names and you'd swallow it, you know damn well you would. But I don't know for sure which one it is, and I'm trying to play this square. I *want* you to go gunning! That'd work out fine for me, you know what I mean?"

"All right."

"I'll find out which one it was. I'll have him fingered definite by the time you want to leave. I swear my oath on that."

"All right."

"Shake on it!"

I shook his hand. When he left, I finished the other bottle.

Nineteen

Monday afternoon we left Plattsburg. The Friday before, Kapp had had a lot of funds transferred to a local bank from a couple of New York and Jersey City banks, and then he'd taken it all out in cash. Monday we walked into the local Cadillac-Oldsmobile-Buick agency, and Kapp bought the showroom Cadillac for cash. I had to drive, because he didn't have a license. I was getting more and more used to judging perspective with just the left eye, and after a while I found a way to get my right foot comfortable on the accelerator, so it wasn't too bad.

We drove straight south to Lake George, and Kapp rented a place around on the eastern side of the lake. The south and west, he said, were all built up from what he'd known, he didn't like it. Over on the northeast, it wasn't much different from the old days.

The house was big and white, built amid evergreens on a steep slope down to the edge of the lake. There was a dirt road along the top of the slope past the summer houses, and a cleared space beside it for two cars to park. We got out of the Cadillac and walked across the tire ruts of the road to the hedge that bordered it for this section. There was a gate in the hedge, and a Quonset-hut mailbox on an arm. On the side of the mailbox was written REED. We'd rented from an agency in town who handled the property for the Reeds off-season. The spaced summer houses along the slope between the road and the lake were all empty, except for us.

We opened the gate in the hedge and went down twelve wooden steps to a screen door and a screened-in porch. On this side, the house looked small. One story high, and just a small screened-in porch with beer and soft drink cases stacked up against the house wall. But this was the top floor of three, the other two sprouting below us down the slope.

Inside, there were three large rooms, all with straw-mat rugs and bamboo or wicker furniture and a lot of dark red cushions. The flooring gleamed rich and well-cared-for in the wide archways between the rooms. There was also a kitchen, white and glittering like an operating room for midgets, with a window overlooking the empty beer cases on the porch. In the middle of it all was a railinged oblong hole in the floor and a staircase with black rubber runners. This led down to the middle floor, where there were four bedrooms, all done in walnut, with little green curtains over the small windows.

There were windows at the front and sides, and a side door which led to a path running down the slope from the road to the lake. There was another set of stairs under the first, this one closed off with knotty pine and a varnished door. It led down to the bottom floor, with storage rooms and the boathouse and another screened porch. Off this porch was a square wooden dock beside the boathouse. The whole house was ringed by trees on three sides, and the fourth side was built right down to the water's edge.

We moved in and found the phone wasn't working, but it was too late that day to do anything about it. The next morning, we drove back around the lake to town and got the phone company to activate the phone. Some sort of belated summer had come in during the night, so I bought a bathing suit. Then we went back to the house.

We didn't talk to each other much, going or coming. Kapp was full of his plans. I was already losing my patience. It was the same as doing the tape for Beeworthy, only that hadn't been any more than half an hour, and this was going to be for two weeks. I wasn't sure I'd last two weeks. The only thing that kept me there was the sure knowledge that it would take me longer than two weeks to get the name I wanted if I was just bulling around New York on my own. I'd told Bill I didn't want to do any Pacific campaign. I still felt the same way.

There was a full-length mirror on the closet door in the bedroom I'd picked for myself. That afternoon, when I put the bathing suit on, I looked at myself in it. It was two and a half months since the accident, and this was the first time I'd really looked at myself full length.

Both shins were criss-crossed with white scars down to the ankles. The right ankle looked wrong. A couple of bones were missing from it, and the doctors had had to rebuild it a little. It was too thin and too smooth. It looked more like a pipe joint than part of a human body. There were more of the white scars above my right knee and across my belly and over my right shoulder.

I opened the closet door all the way, so the mirror was against the wall. I kept it that way from then on. Then I went out and went swimming.

It stayed warm all the rest of the first week. I swam a lot, always by myself. Kapp spent most of his time on the phone. He made a lot of long distance calls to New York and to Miami and to East St. Louis and other places. After the first couple of days, he started getting other calls coming back. He did a lot of grinning and winking, whenever he saw me. But we didn't talk much. I didn't know what he was doing, and I didn't care. And he was too busy with his plans for small talk.

We'd stocked up with House of Lords, and he usually had a glass in his hand. He was smoking cigars all the time, and his voice was getting raspy. He seemed pleased with life.

The air was warm, but the water was cold. I liked it. I couldn't swim as well as before, because I couldn't kick with any coordination, but I did pretty well.

I developed a swimming routine. Every time I went into the water, I swam straight out into the lake as far as I could go. Then I rolled over on my back and rested there until I had the strength to swim back. Sometimes I thought about diving down and walking on the bottom. But not seriously.

They say the Army is hurry up and wait. Air Force, too. When I was in, we used to bitch about that. On an alert, double-time to the truck and climb aboard and then sit and wait for two hours before the truck got moving. I felt now like I used to in the truck, except now the Air Force wasn't doing it to me, I was doing it to myself.

I wanted to *act*. But I didn't want it to be finished. Once I acted and it was over with and I'd done what I'd set out to do, then there wouldn't be anything for me at all any more. A walk on the bottom, it didn't matter at all.

I had trouble sleeping nights. I kept some House of Lords by the bed to help. And the light was always on. I spent a lot of time staring at the ceiling. I hadn't wanted any of this. The things I was doing to myself were as bad as the things they'd done to me. But I couldn't go back. July twelfth was back there, the last good day Ray Kelly had ever had, and I couldn't get back to it. I had to keep moving the other way, hoping there was a way out at the other end.

Toward the end of the week, Kapp came to me and said, "We're going to have to go into town and do some shopping. Some people are coming up. Maybe Monday, Tuesday of next week. I got the list."

We bought groceries, and a lot of beer, and more House of Lords. We also got four Army cots and some cheap blankets and pillows. When we got back the phone was ringing. It rang all weekend. Kapp chewed his cigars to shreds. He was smiling all the time now, like a winner. Even when he was just sitting still, he was doing something. I envied him.

The warm spell broke on Saturday. A sudden wind came down out of the north, turning the lake choppy gray. We closed the windows, and turned on the electric heating units in all the rooms. The sun rectangles were gone from the straw rugs. In the sky, the clouds hurried south.

Sunday, I put on a sweater and went for a walk on the dirt road. It was quiet. Under the evergreens the ground was brown. I thought it would be nice to walk among the trees forever. I'd like to be an Indian, before the white man came.

The phone had been ringing when I left, and it was ringing again when I came back. I carried a folding chair down and sat on the dock and looked out over the lake. That night, the phone stopped ringing.

Monday the first one came. It was in the middle of the afternoon, and I was pouring us fresh drinks in the kitchen. A car horn sounded for just a second. I looked up the slope past the trees and the hedge and saw the side windows of the car and a face under a chauffeur's cap. I said, "Somebody here."

Kapp came around the table and stood beside me. He said, "Go see who it is."

I hopped up the steps and through the gate and over to the car. It was a pearl gray Cadillac, like McArdle's hearse. Three men were bulky in back. The chauffeur was a black cap and a round large nose. He kept both hands on the wheel, high up, and didn't look at me.

I went past him and bent and looked in the side window. The man in the middle said, "Let's see Eddie Kapp."

I said, "He wants to know who you are."

"Nick Rovito."

I went down and told him and he said, "Okay." Then he went out, slamming the screen door, and shouted, "Hey, Nick!"

Up in the car, one of them shouted, "Is that you, you son of a bitch?" Then car doors slammed, and I saw the chauffeur maneuver the car out of the road.

The three men came down. They all looked alike. In their fifties, barrel-bodied, bull-necked, heavy-headed. Wearing tight topcoats, keeping their hands in their pockets. Smiling with thick lips and thin eyes. Rovito stuck his hand out and Kapp shook it. The other two grinned and nodded at Kapp, and he grinned and nodded back. Then they came in.

Rovito looked at me and said, "What's your name?"

"Ray Kelly."

He looked at me and pursed his lips and put his hands back in his topcoat pockets. Then he turned to Kapp and said, "Mmm." It seemed to mean, "I'll let you know."

Kapp said, "Come on in and have a drink. House of Lords."

One of the others said, "Not for me. Doctor's orders." He looked embarrassed.

Rovito looked at him. "Do you still know how to pour?"

"Sure, Nick."

"Then pour."

They went into the living room and sat down. I stayed with them. But they talked about old times and the people they used to know. No one paid any attention to me at all. I went downstairs and out on the dock. They had a window open above me, I could hear the drone of their conversation but not the words.

After fifteen or twenty minutes, the one whose doctor wouldn't let him drink came out on the dock and stood leaning against the side of the boathouse. He lit a cigarette and threw the match in the water and looked at nothing across the water for a couple minutes. Then he turned to me and said, "You're gimpy, aren't you?"

I said, "Yes."

"Fall off your scooter?"

I looked at him. He was grinning. I said, "No."

"Oh," he said. "I see. You don't talk much, do you? You're the strong silent type."

I hadn't heard any voices from upstairs for the last couple minutes. But I didn't look up. I got to my feet and folded the chair and hit him in the stomach with it. He bent over and I hit him on the back of the head with it. When he fell I rolled him off into the water. Then I looked up at the watching faces and said, "Satisfied?"

Kapp was grinning. So was the other guy. Rovito nodded. He said, "So-so."

I started to go inside. Rovito called, "Hey, what about Joe?"

I looked up. "What about him?"

"Aren't you gonna help him out of the water?"

"No. I wasn't playing. I don't play." Then I went in and up to my room and got the bottle from under the bed.

I heard them go by, on their way down to help Joe out of the water.

Twenty

Two more came Monday night, and the phone rang a few times, announcing more who were staying at motels around on the other side of the lake. By Tuesday afternoon, ten of them had moved into the house. I spent most of the time in my room. Whenever anyone opened the door by mistake, they said, "Oh, excuse me," and backed out again. Nobody asked me who I was, and I wasn't introduced to anybody. But they knew.

Appalachin had taught a lesson, though these weren't the same people. But they came in on different highways from different directions. No two cars stopped at the same restaurant or the same motel. They traveled in no convoys.

Wednesday night, eleven o'clock, they had the meeting. Cadillacs clogged the road. Only two of them had New York plates. One had Florida, and one California. Some of the chauffeurs stayed with the cars, some came down to the house.

The two large rooms facing the lake on the top floor had been fixed up for the meeting. All the chairs and tables from all over the house were in those rooms, plus all the ashtrays and wastebaskets. The refrigerator was full of nothing but beer and ice. House of Lords lined the cupboards. The early arrivals played poker while they waited.

Kapp came down to my room at ten-thirty. He was wearing one of the black suits he'd bought in Plattsburg. His shirt was white and his tie was black. Tie and collar were both too wide and too pointed. So were his shoes, which were black. The ring on his left pinky was white gold. His cigar was black. A white handkerchief peeked out of his breast pocket. His gray hair was brushed back till it shone. He didn't exactly look fatter, but he did look sort of heavier, as though he were more solid, more full.

He said, "The big moment, eh, boy?" He was like an actor, all made up in his starchy costume, ready to go on.

He sat down on the edge of the bed and looked at the empty bottle standing beside the ashtray on the floor. He said, "You aren't juiced, are you?"

"No."

"Good. I want to give you a rundown on these people."

I lit a cigarette and waited. If he felt like talking, I could listen.

He said, "There's thirty-eight people going to be here, not counting you and me. Nick Rovito and Irving Baumheiler and Little Irving Stein are here because I'm here. There's seven other guys here because those three are. And twelve more here because of the seven. And sixteen because of the twelve. You see?"

I nodded.

"The point is, it's Nick and Irving and Little Irving you got to watch for. Those three. By you, they're the only ones here. Nick Rovito and Irving Baumheiler and Little

Irving Stein. You met them, right?"

"Not the last one. Little Irving."

"Oh. Little guy, baldheaded. You'll recognize him."

"All right."

"Fine. Now, all you do is stay with me. You don't have to talk unless you feel like it. The less said the better, maybe. But stick with me, at least till the talking's done. You got to pee, do it now."

I shook my head.

"You sure?"

"Goddamn it."

"Okay, okay. Just so you know. You got to stay right with me. Right side, you see? On my right side."

"All right."

"You got your brother's Luger?"

"The other one's smaller. The revolver."

"Where is it?"

I pointed at the dresser. "Top drawer."

"Wear it. Where you can reach it, where you can show it. But not where you can't hide it. You know what I mean?"

"In my belt, at the side."

"Okay, fine." He stood up, smoothed the wrinkles out of his jacket and trousers. I reached off the bed for the ashtray and put it on my chest. He said, "Don't get me wrong. Nobody's going to shoot nobody. But maybe somebody wants to know if you're carrying, you see? And you are."

"Okay."

He walked around the room, blowing cigar smoke like a big cattleman. "There's two kinds of people in this world, Ray," he said. "There are leaders, and there are followers. And there's only the one kind of follower, but there's all kinds of leaders. There's glorious leaders that take a whole goddamn country over the cliff, and there's ward leaders that wouldn't last a day without the snow-shovel patronage. And all kinds of leaders in between, you see what I mean?"

"I see what you mean." It was a phrase I'd heard him use before. He was talking now because he was nerved up. I didn't even have to make believe I was listening.

"Now most of these guys that are going to be here tonight," he said, "they're what you might call middle-ground leaders. They can lead a bunch of followers fine, just so long as somebody else tells them how. Somebody else like Nick and Irving and Little Irving, you know what I mean?"

I looked up at the ceiling and blew cigarette smoke at it. The ashtray rode my chest. Kapp prowled around the room, talking to let off steam. "Most of these guys," he said, "these middle-ground leaders, they've been around straight on through since the thirties. But their top men, like Nick and the Irvings, they've been out of commission for a while. So the rest of these guys have just drifted. Some of them are with the mob now, way down at the bottom of the list, where the crumbs fall. They'll be here, because they want to move up a notch. And they figure Nick or one of the Irvings for their real boss anyway, not one of these thin, slick snotnoses like they have today. So there they are, they've already got a little chunk of the organization in their pocket. When the time comes, they consolidate that chunk and then maybe send a couple arms to help straighten out some other neighborhood somewhere. See what I mean?"

"Yeah." I moved the ashtray off my chest and sat up for a while.

"And the other kind of guy we'll see," he said, "is the independent. New York's a big apple. There's independents working right inside the city limits, not even paying off to the regular organization. A neighborhood book, a little quiet unionizing, one thing and another. All off in little corners, out in Brooklyn and Queens. Small-time leaders again. They want to be part of the mob, if Nick and the Irvings and me are running it."

"Yeah."

"We got half an organization already," he said. "All we do is grab the other half. Like plucking a peach." He laughed. "You know what I mean? Like plucking a peach."

Over our heads people were walking back and forth. Kapp looked up at the ceiling. "I better go up," he said. "You come up as soon as you can."

"Yeah."

He went to the door and opened it. Then he looked back at me and closed it again and said, "You sore at something, boy?"

"Nothing special."

He shook his head and grinned at me. "You're a surly bastard," he said.

"I'm the strong silent type."

He widened his eyes. "You sore about that little trick on the dock?"

"No." I swung my legs over the side. "The hell with it.

I'm not sore at anything." I put the ashtray on the dresser and got out Smitty's gun. It was full again. The barrel was cold.

"Get dressed up sharp," Kapp told me.

"Yeah, yeah."

"Surly as they come." He went out, grinning and shaking his head.

I put on a dark gray suit and a light gray tie and black shoes. Square shirt collar. I stuck Smitty's gun inside my belt around on the left side, with the butt forward. So I could reach over with my right hand and get it. Then I went upstairs.

Most of them were there. The archway between the two rooms was wide, almost as wide as the rooms. The chairs were set up informally around the two rooms, but so that everybody could see everybody else and nobody had their back to anybody else. The poker players had quit. People in tight suits and fat grins were shaking hands and showing their teeth. Three chauffeurs were doubling as bartenders, bringing glasses of beer or House of Lords out from the kitchen. All thirty-eight were talking. Most of them were smoking cigars. The rest were smoking cigarettes. I lit one myself and went around the wall to Kapp. He was with Rovito and a little baldheaded guy with a big nose.

Kapp put his arm around my shoulders and said, "You remember Nick."

"Sure."

We nodded at each other, and Rovito smiled first.

Kapp motioned the cigar hand at the other one. "And this is—"

"Little Irving Stein," I said. I nodded at him. "Nice to meet you."

"You reckanize me? Sure, why not?" He poked Kapp's elbow. "Did I tell you? I got a broad works for me, she does nothin' but read books for a mention of Little Oiving. I put the covers on the living room wall. Mostly paperbacks, you know? Half the wall I got already. You think they forgot? Nobody forgot, don't let 'em kid you. They're still grateful, Ed, they still got a soft spot in their hearts for the selfless bums kept them in booze all those years in the desert. Ain't that right, Nick?"

Nick showed teeth, and didn't quite look down at Little Irving. Kapp said, "Well, the hell, let's get going." He turned and put his cigar on the edge of an ashtray and then straightened again and clapped his hands. "Cell and block!" he shouted. "Cell and block!"

A lot of people laughed, and then it got quiet.

Kapp said, "Let's all sit down, what do you say?"

It was the same as any bunch of people at a meeting. Chairs squeaking around, people finishing conversations. Then there was the last cough, and silence.

There were five of us standing, thirty-five of them seated. Kapp leaned against the archway between the rooms, his arms folded and his cigar pointing at the ceiling. I stood to his right and back just a little. Nick Rovito stood leaning against the wall near the corner diagonally to my right. Irving Baumheiler, a very fat man in a vest with his thumb in the vest pocket, stood behind a chair facing me, midway between Nick and the opposite side of the arch. Against the far wall in the other room stood Little Irving Stein.

Except for me, there wasn't a man in the room under fifty-five. Most of them were the other side of sixty. Gray hair, dyed hair, and no hair. Half of them in new out-of-date clothes. All of them watching, smoking, waiting.

Kapp motioned to one of the chauffeurs, in the doorway to the kitchen. He came over with a tray and Kapp took a House of Lords. So did I. It was quiet.

Kapp broke the silence. He looked at the full glass in his hand and said, "There's a lot to tell in this little glass. What's in it made a lot of guys a lot of dough. People who didn't want it said nobody else should have it, and then it made some other people even more dough." He grinned at the glass. "Or maybe the same people, who knows? I made my share out of it when they said it wasn't legal. Then they grabbed me for not splitting with them on money they didn't want me to make. And said it was legal after all. And then I went to a place where they didn't serve it, legal or otherwise. Fifteen years without a drop, boys. That's a hell of a long trip to take on a water wagon."

It was a water-glass, half full. He downed it in three swallows, and tossed it empty, underhand, across the room to the chauffeur in the doorway. Nick Rovito said, low, "Get on with it, Eddie."

"That was the ceremony, Nick. The christening. Gents, I want you to meet my boy. My son, goes by the name of Ray Kelly." Then he pointed the cigar at face after face in a counterclockwise circle around the room, and called off the name of every man there.

I watched for the first seven, my blank face and their blank faces, and then the hell with it. I drank the House of

Lords from eight to twenty-one, turned and put down the empty glass on a table from twenty-two to twenty-four, lit a cigarette till thirty-three, and watched the last five. "And that, Nick," he finished, "was the introduction."

Nick didn't say anything. He didn't move.

Kapp inhaled cigar smoke and blew it out again. "They said liquor was illegal," he said, talking to the smoke this time, "and then they said it wasn't. But a lot of money was made while it was. Now, who knows what else they may decide is legal? How about Mary Jane? Ray, what do they call it now? Marijuana."

"Pot," I said.

"Ugly. All right, what about it? No after-effects, less habit-forming than tobacco or liquor. Maybe we'll wake up one morning and it's legal."

A guy to the left muttered, "They better not." A few others laughed.

Kapp nodded at him. "Yeah, Sal, I know what you mean. The same with off-track horse betting, huh? Or all of gambling, like Nevada. All over the country. Maybe so, some day. Or whores in ghettos, like they tried in Galveston and some other places."

Little Irving said, "What's the point, Eddie?"

"The point? I don't see why we shouldn't figure it all legal right now, that's the point. Retroactive, you know what I mean? Like their stinking income taxes. You see what I mean?"

They grinned and nodded and shifted around in their chairs, relaxing, puffing on their stogies, grinning at one another. Nick grinned, too. He said, "And that was the joke, huh, Eddie?"

Kapp said, "Right you are, Nick. And now we get to the pie."

They quieted again. Kapp said, "Let's get the size of the pie straight. It isn't the country. It isn't the east. It's New York City. And the stuff around it, Jersey City and Long Island and the rest."

Somebody said, "Greater New York."

"That's the word."

Somebody else said, "Why so modest, Eddie?"

Kapp said, "You tell them, Irving."

Baumheiler cleared his throat and took his thumb out of his vest pocket. He said, "I mention to you gentlemen five names. Arnold Greenglass. Salvatore Abbadarindi. Edward Wiley. Sean Auchinachie. Vito Petrone. These gentlemen are old friends of ours, of most of ours. They are our contemporaries, more fortunate than we in not having had their careers interrupted in the late thirties or early forties. They would still be considered our friends. They, and others of our friends, are now operative at the national and regional levels. They agree with us that we deserve Greater New York more than the group that now has it, contingent of course on our proving our ability by taking it from the incumbents. National and regional organizations, as well as local organizations from other centers, will not interfere in the struggle. We have their assurances on this point. This is based on our own assurances that we harbor no ambitions beyond Greater New York."

"For the moment," said the guy who'd spoken up before.

Baumheiler looked severely at him. "For ever," he

said. "We are not, and will not be, a rival organization. We are part of the existent organization, and shall continue to be so."

Little Irving Stein said to the ambitious one, "You ought to know better, Kenny."

Kenny, who was at least as old as Stein and twice the size, shifted uneasily in his chair. "I just wanted to get it straight," he said.

Kapp said, "If we made a move like we wanted a bigger pie, they'd stop us from getting any pie at all. And they could, any time they wanted. Right, Nick?"

Nick nodded heavily. "That's right," he said. "My people understood that already."

"Mine do, now," said Little Irving. He glared at Kenny.

Kapp said, "We know who these punks are, this bunch that Irving called the incumbents. We know them from the old days, right? They shined our shoes in the old days, am I right?"

Somebody said, "Office boys."

"That's the word," said Kapp. "Office boys. Soft easy-living punks. They ain't in the rackets, they're a bunch of businessmen. You know what I mean? They live quiet, they send each other inter-office memos. They're a bunch of accountants. Am I right?"

Most of them nodded or said, "You're right."

"Accountants," repeated Kapp. "Office boys. They're afraid of muscle, they're afraid of the noisy hit. A quiet hit is what they like, an old lady's hit. Arsenic in the five o'clock tea, you know what I mean?"

They laughed.

"Sure," said Kapp. He was laughing with them. "An old lady's hit. They're a bunch of old ladies. They're *soft*. They hear a loud noise, they think it's a backfire. On the payroll they don't have even one good demo man. Huh? Am I right?"

"The only bombs thrown around New York," said somebody, "are by amateurs."

"We ought to hire them, that's what I say," said Kapp. He got a laugh on that one, too. A bunch of old friends, getting set up together, getting along.

Kapp motioned to the chauffeur in the kitchen doorway. "Time for a round," he said.

Glasses came around and everybody was noisy for a minute, and then Kapp said, "As I was saying." Silence. He smiled into it. "As I was saying, these pretty people are soft. They're *soft*. Do they know we're coming? Sure they do. Are they scared? So scared, boys, they've been using the noisy hit. I swear to God. They've been trying for Ray here, for my boy. They gunned his foster father, Will Kelly. You boys remember Will Kelly."

They all agreed, they remembered Will Kelly.

Kapp said, "They tried to gun me, too, on my way out of D. Ever hear of anybody *try* to gun somebody? They missed! They don't even know how!"

Nick Rovito said, "We've got the point, Eddie."

"I want to be sure of that," Kapp told him. "We aren't up against people like the Gennas or Lepke or any of Albert A's boys or anybody like that. We're up against a bunch of bush leaguers. We're up against a goddamn P.T.A. Okay." He became suddenly brisker, more businesslike. "Okay," he said. "They're in, and we're out. And we're not gonna get in *their* way. We're gonna get in *our* way, or not at all."

Baumheiler said, "Remember Dewey, Ed. You do not want to stir things up too much."

"How much does it take, Irving? We want them out. We want us in. How much do we have to stir to get what we want? I promise you, I won't stir any more than that."

Baumheiler chewed slowly on his cigar. "I don't like the idea of too much noise, Eddie," he said. "Bombs going off, lots of bullets, lots and lots of hits. I don't like such an idea. And I am not an old lady."

Nick Rovito said, "What worries you, Irving?"

"Noise, Mr. Rovito. I do not—"

"You can call me Nick, Irving."

"Thank you, Mr. Rovito. I do not like—"

Kapp said, "Irving, are we going to get along here or aren't we?"

"We can discuss the situation, Eddie, surely."

"On a first-name basis, Irving. When we're back in, you and Nick can hate each other some more. But right now we got to work together."

"We've always been able to work together in the past," said Baumheiler, with a side glance at Nick, "despite our differences."

"Stick with first names, Irving. We're all old friends."

Baumheiler shrugged heavy shoulders. "If you think best, Eddie, then of course. To answer your question— Nick—I do not like noise. I do not like the idea of the State Crime Commission handing me a subpoena. I do not like the idea of being hauled, like Frank Costello, before a televised Congressional investigation. I do not like the idea of Federal accountants interesting themselves overmuch in my affairs. This is a different time, a different world. Our former associates are not used to noise, I agree. However, the citizenry is equally unused to noise. We would find them perhaps less tolerant than was once the case. I recommend circumspection."

"No citizens, Irving," said Kapp. "But hits. Bombs, and you know it. We got no choice."

"Quiet hits, maybe," said Nick. "But not poison in the tea. Lead in the head, huh? Not *too* quiet, huh, Irving? We want them to know maybe we're there, huh?"

"I simply want it made clear that I would not personally appreciate the type of over-enthusiasm which put our lamented friend Lepke in the electric chair."

The porch door opened. A chauffeur stuck his head in and said, "There's a car pulled up. A dinge in the back, he says he wants to talk."

In the silence, I moved out from the wall, saying, "I'll go see what he wants."

They watched me go. Nobody talked.

Twenty-One

It was a black Chrysler Imperial. Amid the Cadillacs, it looked belligerent. There was a white chauffeur and a black rider. He was no more than thirty, dressed out of Brooks Brothers on an expense account. A gold Speidel band was on his watch, a gold wedding band on the third finger of his left hand. He had a chicken mustache and a small satisfied smile and two watchful eyes.

When I got there, he pressed a button and the window slid down. The side and back windows had black Venetian blinds. The others were down, the one on this side was up. He looked out at me and said, "I'm from Ed Ganolese. With a proposition for Anthony Kapp."

I said, "All right, messenger. Come on down and say your piece."

He got gracefully out of the Chrysler. I led the way. Behind me, he said, "Don't you want to frisk me? What if I were armed?"

"What if you were?"

We went down the steps. At the door I turned and said, "What name? I'll introduce you."

"William Cheever."

"Princeton?"

He smiled. "Sorry. Tuskegee."

I didn't smile back. We went in, through the empty room, with chauffeurs showing guns in the kitchen on our right, and on to where the piemen waited. I stopped in the archway and said, "Mister William Cheever. Of Tuskegee. With a message from Ed Ganolese." Then I went over and stood beside Kapp.

Cheever's smile was faint and phony. He nodded at the room, took note of the five standing men, and then looked at the one beside me. "Anthony Kapp?"

"I'm called Eddie. Not by you."

"Mr. Kapp, then. I have been sent, as of course you assume, to discuss terms. My principals—"

"You mean Ed Ganolese, that two-bit bum."

"Ed Ganolese, yes. He sent me with a proposition concer—"

Kapp said, "No."

Nick Rovito said, "Wait a second, Eddie. Let's hear what he's got to say."

"I don't care what he's got to say," said Kapp. "Ganolese and his sidekicks are in my territory. That's all I have to know."

"You can't listen to him?"

"No. I can't. Look, Nick, they got the pie, am I right? There's only the one pie, and they got it. If we had it, and this bum came in and said his principals wanted some of it, what would we do?"

"We don't have it," Nick said. "That's the point."

"And they won't give us any more than we'd give them."

Nick spread his hands. "We can talk, can't we?"

"We can go to the movies, too, Nick. We can scratch our asses. There's lots of ways to waste time."

"You don't want to ride me, Eddie."

Little Irving Stein piped up, "Ganolese couldn't of asked for better. Throw one spade on the table and watch everybody fold."

Nick said, "Oh, the hell with it. All right, Eddie, you're right."

"Okay, fine." Kapp looked at Cheever. "What the hell you still doing here? You got your answer. No deal."

Little Irving said, "Why don't we send this buck back with pennies on his eyes? So they'll know we mean it."

Baumheiler said, "No. They already know it."

Little Irving said, "Come on. We got ourselves here a little Fort Sumter."

Baumheiler said, "It's just such noisiness as this that I have in mind. I consider it dangerous."

Nick said to Cheever, "Go on, little man, you better go home."

Cheever opened his mouth. Kapp said, "Move!" He shrugged and nodded and went out, gathering the sheepskin folds of his dignity about him as he went. He closed the door and somebody said, disgustedly, "A deuce."

"Like I said," Kapp told them, "they're all deuces. I believe we were splitting the pie, boys, before the dark cloud blew in." Sometime, he'd started a new cigar. He clenched it, and talked through it. "I figure to do this democratic," he said. "What we're going to need at the outset is enforcers. Lots of them. And trustworthy. Not deuces like that one, that'll go running back to Ganolese all of a sudden. And the boys that bring in the most arms get the most gravy. You see what I mean?"

"You mean a redistribution, Eddie?" asked Nick.

"Not at our level, Nick. We work the same as always. You've got Long Island and Brooklyn and Queens, Irving has Jersey and Staten Island, and Little Irving has the Bronx and Westchester. And the four of us operate Manhattan together. Same as we discussed, right?"

"Then what's this talk about gravy?"

"Down in the neighborhoods, Nick. There's gonna have to be a redistribution in the neighborhoods. There's a lot of disloyal types we've got to replace, you know what I mean?"

Nick nodded. "All right," he said. "That sounds like an incentive for the rest of you guys, huh?"

There was scattered agreement, and Kapp said, "Okay, so let's talk about arms. How many and where. And how much capital do we need to get rolling."

Two or three of them started talking at once, telling about athletic clubs and veteran's organizations and other things, and Kapp smoked while the three top men argued with their assistants.

I didn't care how they sliced their pie. I walked through them to the kitchen and got a bottle of House of Lords and went downstairs and got my folding chair out of my bedroom and brought it down to the dock.

There was a cold wind ruffling the sea and blowing away the words of the peasant kings upstairs. But the wall of the boathouse protected me from most of it. The sky was dark and the lake darker. I sat and smoked and held the bottle till it was warm and wet in my fingers. Then I drank from it and set it down on the warped white wood beside the chair.

After a while, the door opened behind me and Kapp came out. I could still hear the voices upstairs. Kapp came over, grinning, trailing gray cigar smoke, and said, "It's coming along, huh, Ray?"

"I guess it is," I said.

"And all on account of you. Now, we all got together, we got a firm base here, you know what I mean?"

"Is Ganolese the one?"

"You figured that, huh? I thought you did. Yeah, if he's the one making the propositions, then he's the one ordered the guns."

"That's what I thought."

He walked out to the end of the dock, looked out into the darkness a minute, and then turned and winked at me, grinning. He glanced up at the lighted windows on the top floor, where his staff was readying his army, and then he walked back to me and said, "You bring me luck, Ray. I didn't figure it to run this smooth. Only a little trouble between Nick and Irving, everybody else coming along nice. We can't miss, boy."

"Nick and Irving don't like each other, huh?"

"They hate each other's guts. Always have. But they work together. It's the way of the world, you know what I mean?"

"I know."

He walked around the dock some more, and then said, "You figure to go after Ganolese, huh?"

"Uh huh."

"But there's no hurry, right? You're better off, you wait a while. You see what I mean?"

"No, I don't."

"Pretty soon, Ganolese is gonna have full hands. We're gonna hit his bunch of bastards so hard and so often he won't know which way is Aqueduct. That's the time for you to slip in at him, right? When he's too busy to see you coming."

"I guess so."

"Take it from me. I know the way these things work."

"Maybe you're right."

"Sure. One more thing. What did you think of the spade?"

"Cheever? Nothing at all. What should I think?"

"I wondered if you picked that up," he said. "But maybe you wouldn't. You don't have the background for it."

"Pick what up?"

He stood there and unwrapped a cigar. "It's this way," he said. "A mob, an organization like this, it's in some ways like a business, you know what I mean? Lots of details, lots of executives and vice-presidents, people in charge of this and that and the other thing, you see? No one man running the whole thing."

I nodded. "All right."

"Now Ganolese," he said, "he's the one pointed the finger at you, and Will Kelly, and your brother, and your sister-in-law. But he wouldn't have thought it up all by himself. The word would come in, Eddie Kapp's planning a move and thus and so, and somebody would go up to Ganolese and tell him the situation and make a suggestion. Do this or that, boss, and the whole thing is clear."

"Cheever?"

He paused, looking out at the lake while he lit his cigar. Still looking out that way, he said, "And when an operation falls apart, it's the guy who suggested that operation in the first place who gets any dirty jobs that might come up because of the failure. Like carrying messages to the enemy. Things like that."

"I see."

"I thought you might want to know," he said. "I thought maybe you wouldn't pick it up."

"I didn't."

He chewed on the cigar, looking at me out of the corner of his eye. After a minute, he said, "You remember what we were talking about in Plattsburg, family and respectability?"

"I remember."

"This is about Cheever again. The Negro. He wants to be respectable, too, same as everybody else. But he can't be, and it don't matter how many generations he's been here, you see what I mean? So he's liable to wind up in the organization. If he's smart and he's got a good education and he's tough, he's liable to get himself a good position in the organization. Better than he could get outside."

"Us minorities got to stick together," I said.

He laughed. "Yeah, boy, I like you. But I was making a point. About family. The Negro, see, he's got the respectability itch, same as the Italian or the Jew or the Irishman or the Greek, but he don't have the same itch about family, you know what I mean? He's had that part sold out of him. Brought over here as slaves, Papa sold here, Mama sold there, kids sold up and down the river. And it wasn't so long ago the selling stopped."

"A hundred years," I said.

"That ain't long. He still ain't gonna get dewy-eyed over somebody else's family. That's another point to consider."

"Yeah, I see that."

"It's nice up here," he said suddenly. He inhaled noisily, blew breath out at the lake. "I figure to stick around a while, a week or so, till things get moving. You ought to wait till then, anyway. Why not stay here?"

"I hadn't thought about it," I said.

"We get to know each other," he said. "Father and son. What do you say?"

I shrugged. "I don't know. I'll think about it."

He patted my shoulder. "You do that. We can talk about it tomorrow. You coming back up?"

"You need me?"

"Not unless you want to come. This is just the business meeting now."

"I'll stay here a while."

"Okay. See you in the morning."

"Sure."

He went inside. I heard him going up the stairs. I sat a while longer, looking out at the lake. After a while, I tossed the bottle off the end of the dock and went back up to my room. I packed the suitcase and went out the side door and up the slope toward the road. They were all still talking back there in the throne room.

I told a chauffeur, "You're supposed to drive me into town."

He did, and I found the Greyhound station. I waited in the diner across the street until the New York bus came. Then I got aboard and went to sleep.

Twenty-Two

I awoke at Hudson, with the dim gray of pre-dawn on the bus windows. It was sprinkling, and the long wipers smacked back and forth across the windshield. I sat midway down the aisle, on the right side. There were only about four other passengers. I had both seats all the way back and I was sprawled at an angle on them, head against the windowpane and shoeless feet in the aisle. I was cramped and muggy. I'd been in that position too long. I felt like wet wool.

What woke me up, the bus had stopped. A man came running across the sidewalk from the store-front bus depot. He had a slick black raincoat draped over his head. The driver pushed the door open and the other man stood in the gutter, and they shouted back and forth over the sound of the rain. Then the man turned and ran back in, and the driver closed the door, and we started out of Hudson. They always do that, whenever it rains. I don't know what they say to one another.

I couldn't get back to sleep. I was sitting on the wrong side to see the dawn, so I looked out at the darkness and wished the bus were going to Binghamton.

It got lighter and lighter outside the window. The towns passed by. Red Hook and Rhineland and back across the river to Kingston. Then West Park and Highland and across the river again to Poughkeepsie. Then Wappingers Falls and Fishkill and Beacon, Peekskill and Ossining and Tarrytown, White Plains and Yonkers and New York.

I got off at 50th Street. I walked a ways and went into the Cuttington Hotel on 52nd Street.

They would all be looking for me now, so I'd have to register under a phony name. Walking up from the bus terminal, I chose Matthew Allen. A reasonable but for-gettable name, and it didn't use my initials.

Stupid things happen. I got terrified when the register was turned toward me. I'd never given a false name before. My hand shook as I wrote the name, so bad it wasn't my writing at all. And I couldn't look the woman desk clerk in the eye. She spent a lot of time explaining to me that I was signing in at an unusual hour and she would have to charge me for last night because the day ended at three p.m. I told her it was all right, and got away from her as soon as I could, following the bellboy.

Once in the room, alone, it struck me funny. After all that had happened, to practically faint when I had to write a phony name. I lay down on the bed and laughed, and the laughter got out of control. Down in a corner of my mind the laughing frightened me. Then the laughter got mixed around and turned upside down and I was crying. Then I laughed because it was funny to be crying, and cried because it was sad to be laughing. When I was empty, I fell asleep.

I woke up at one with smarting feet. I hadn't taken my shoes off. I stripped and showered, and walked around the room naked while the last of the stiffness went away. Then I got dressed, and sat down at the writing table, and wrote a little letter to my Uncle Henry, telling him to write me as Matthew Allen at this hotel. Not in care of Matthew Allen, but as Matthew Allen. Then I left the room.

I made it to the bank on time, where a little more than half of Bill's three thousand dollars still waited in our joint account to be spent. I took out two hundred, and went to a luncheonette and had breakfast, surrounded by people eating a late lunch. And then I had nothing in the world to do. I bought four paperback books and a deck of cards and went back to the room.

I knew that Kapp was right, that I should wait before

going after Ganolese. If I were to get to him, without myself being killed, it would be better to wait till his attention was distracted. Kapp and his junta would make a fine distraction. Once they had made their move, I could make mine.

The thing was, it wouldn't be sufficient for me to be killed attempting my revenge. I wasn't trying to sacrifice myself. I wanted to come out alive on the other side. So it was best to wait.

But I'm not good at waiting. That first afternoon, I read a while and then I ripped up all four of the books. They were action mysteries, and they were supposed to help me stop thinking about myself. But all they managed to do was keep prodding the open wound I'd been trying to ignore. All they did was remind me that, if all went well, I *would* be alive when this was over. That was the part, most of all, that I didn't want to think about.

Life uses people up. When I was finished with what I had to do, I could hardly be the same person I'd been the day the Air Force had made me a civilian and I had re-met Dad. Who I would be, what use or purpose I might find—I didn't know, and I didn't want to ask. Yet I had to live, or it would be their triumph after all, and my defeat, even if I were to kill them all and then be killed myself, by my hand or theirs.

It was simpler for the lead characters in the books. They suffered, they involved themselves with tense and driven people, they handled sudden death like a commodity in a secondary market. But when it was all finished, they were unchanged. What they had walked through had left no mark at all on them.

It would be nice to believe that. But the writers were blandly lying. They weren't using up their lead character, because they needed him in the next book in the series.

So I went out and bought a bottle of Old Mr. Boston, and on Friday I went to the newspaper library and wasted the day reading about Ed Ganolese. Every once in a while, it seemed, he was served a subpoena and he answered questions before an investigating body of some sort or another. The investigators were always after someone else and usually they asked Ganolese about his relationship with that someone else as of twenty years before. His answers were never informative, but he always managed to be just barely cooperative enough to avoid the legal wrath of the investigators.

Once, there was a photograph. It showed a man somewhat older than fifty, well fed but still strong-looking. He had a kind of brutal handsomeness, softened by time and weight, and the waist-up dignity of the nouveau riche. He sat before a microphone shaped like a hooded snake, and he brooded at his inquisitors.

Another time, a reporter explained that the name was pronounced "Jan-o-lease," and was originally spelled Gianolliese, but the family had shortened and somewhat Anglicized it.

No one had ever done a profile on him.

Friday night, I saw two science-fiction horror movies on 42nd Street. The weekend inched by. Sunday morning, I awoke with a bitter headache at eight o'clock, with less than four hours sleep. But I couldn't drop off again, and it took me an hour to understand why. Then, feeling like a fool, I got up and dressed and found a

Catholic Church, and prayed for Bill, who wasn't here. It wasn't that *I* attended Mass. Bill's stand-in came to Mass, and he was me. When Mass was over, I left with no more interest in the place, my duty done. I went back to the hotel, and to bed, and to sleep.

Starting Monday, I read the papers, all of them. It was five days since the meeting at Lake George. The coup d'etat should begin soon.

It began on Wednesday night. Reading Thursday morning's papers, I nearly missed it. I took a cab back to the hotel from the *Daily News* building on East 42nd Street, where I had bought the Brooklyn and Queens and Bronx editions of that paper. I bought the other morning papers in the hotel lobby and went upstairs and worked my way through them. I sat cross-legged on the bed, turning pages with my left hand, holding the Old Mr. Boston bottle in my right.

I went all the way through, and something was bothering me. Something in the *News*. I took the Queens edition and went through it again, and this time when I came to the candy store explosion I stopped.

It was a small candy store in a bad section of Queens. At ten-thirty last night, a gas heater in the back of the store exploded, killing the proprietor. It was the proprietor's brother, a man named Gus Porophorus, who told the firemen about the gas heater.

There was a photograph of the burned and jumbled back part of the store. The photograph showed a blackboard along one wall.

I got up from the bed and lit a cigarette and walked around the room, laughing. I'd seen posters in subway stations, advertising the *Daily News*. The poster would have a big blowup of an unusual photograph, and the caption, "No one says it like the *News*."

A blackboard in the back room of a candy store! No one says it like the *News*. The horseplayers wouldn't have anywhere to place their bets in that neighborhood for a few days.

I'd been expecting something like the movies. Banner headlines screaming, GANGLAND SLAYING. I'd forgotten what Kapp had said to Irving Baumheiler: "Quiet hits. Hits, but quiet hits."

I went through all the papers again, and this time I knew what to look for. A stationery store fire in the Bronx, owner killed in the blaze. And a man named Anthony Manizetsky, 36, unemployed, killed when his car rammed into a steel support under the West Side Drive at 22nd Street. There was a photo of the car, last year's Buick. And an import firm's warehouse burned down on Third Avenue in Brooklyn.

I got yesterday's papers out of the closet, wondering if I'd missed the opening gun. But I hadn't. It had started last night.

I felt twenty pounds lighter. I had been hating the hotel room. I put the top on the Old Mr. Boston bottle and called Ed Johnson. When I told him who it was he said, "I wondered what happened to you. It's been almost a month now."

I said, "Have they been asking you questions about me any more?"

"No, thank God. Just the one time. I had a tail for about three days after that. He was lousy, but I figured it would be a bad move to lose him. Since he left, nothing at all."

"Good. I've got a job for you, if you want it. Can I trust you?"

"If you think you can trust my answer to that," he said, "you think you can trust me."

"All right. I want a man's address. I want to know where I can find him for sure."

"Is this number one, or are you still poking around?"

"If I don't tell you, you can't tell anybody else."

"All right, I'm not very brave. I don't get paid enough to be brave. What's the name?"

"Ed Ganolese." I spelled it for him. "I'm not sure what the Ed is short for."

"All right. He's in New York, for sure?"

"Somewhere around here. Maybe he commutes."

"Wait a second, I've seen this name somewhere."

"He's one of the people who run the local syndicate."

"Oh. Well—I'm not sure. I can't guarantee anything."

"I know that."

"I'll have to be careful who I ask."

"More than last time."

"I know who it was that time. I wish I had the guts to do something about it. Where do I call you?"

"I'll call you Saturday. Three in the afternoon. At your office."

"I don't blame you," he said. "This isn't my league."

"Then don't kick yourself for it. I'll call you Saturday."

Then I went out and bought a pair of scissors. I came back and clipped the war news.

Twenty-Three

The afternoon papers carried more of it. A boiler explosion in a residence hotel off Eighth Avenue, in the middle of Whore Row. A liquor-store owner shot to death in what the papers called a hold-up attempt, though the "bandit" had stolen nothing—it was suggested that he had been scared off after firing the four shots that had killed the owner. Another fatal automobile accident, this one in Jackson Heights, in which the driver, who had been alone in his year-old Bonneville Pontiac, was listed in the paper as "unemployed."

The coup was less than twenty-four hours old. I had seven clippings. Each separate item was explainable in some manner less dramatic than the truth. No outsider, reading these separate and minor reports from the front, would guess that a revolution was taking place.

Most of the action wouldn't be hitting the papers at all. There were surely men who had disappeared in the last twenty-four hours, and who would never be heard from again, but no one would be calling the police to find them. Other men, insisting that they had fallen downstairs, would be entering hospitals with no more public fanfare than is given any obscure accident victim. Store owners would be gazing gloomily at wrecked showcases and merchandise, about which they would not be calling the police or the insurance company.

Thursday night I walked around Manhattan steadily

for five hours. I avoided midtown and Central Park, so most of my time was spent between 50th and 100th Streets, on and near Broadway. I had no goal. I simply had to burn the energy off. I saw no signs of the struggle.

Friday morning, I added three more clippings. Friday afternoon, I added another five. Among them was a resident of the Riverdale section of the Bronx, who broke his neck when he fell down a flight of stairs in his house. I recognized the name. He was one of the men who'd been at the meeting in Lake George. So the incumbents were fighting back.

The police must know what was going on. But they wouldn't be anxious to advertise it. Like Irving Baumheiler, they would want it all very quiet. No sense upsetting the citizenry.

Saturday morning the papers reported, without knowing it, the results of a major battle the night before. The *News*, the *Mirror* and the *Herald Tribune* all reported the Athletic Club blaze in Brooklyn. The *Herald Tribune* and the *Times* reported the boiler explosion in the East Side night club half an hour after closing. Two more of the Lake George insurgents had run into fatal accidents, one in his home and one in his car. All in all, I had clippings on eleven incidents in the battle, no one of them found sufficiently newsworthy to be mentioned by all four of the morning papers.

When I called Johnson at three, he sounded nervous. "What the hell were you setting me up for, Kelly?"

"Why? What happened?"

"Nothing. I stuck my nose in and pulled it right back out again. Something's going on."

"I know."

"You could've warned me."

"I did. I told you to be careful."

"Listen, just do me one favor. Don't call me any more, okay?"

"All right."

"Whatever the hell it is, I don't want any part of it. I don't even want to know about it."

"All right, Johnson, I understand you. I won't bother you again."

"I'd like to help you out," he said, and now he sounded apologetic. "But this just isn't my league."

"You said that before."

"It's still true. I'm great on divorce."

"In other words, you don't know where Ganolese is."

"I got both his addresses. An apartment in town here, and a house out on the Island. But he isn't at either one of them. And whatever's going on, this doesn't look like a good time to ask where else he might be."

"All right."

"I'm sorry. I did my best."

"I know. Don't worry about it. This shouldn't be anybody's league."

We hung up, and I lit a cigarette and decided I'd have to do it the other way around. I looked in the phone book and found William Cheever's law office listed, but no home phone. He wouldn't be there on Saturday afternoon.

It was a long weekend.

Twenty-Four

Cheever's office was on West 111th Street, the edge of Harlem. Monday morning I took the subway uptown.

I got off at 110th Street, the northwest tip of Central Park, and walked north into the ghetto. I wore my raincoat over my suit, bulky enough so Smitty's gun made no bulge under my belt. It was daytime, so no one looked at me twice.

The building was eight stories tall. A large record store chromed the first floor. The rest of the building, ancient brick and dusty windows, stuck up out of all that chrome and glass and gaiety like a wart.

The door I wanted was off to the left, stuck under the record store's armpit. I went up narrow-canted stairs for three flights, each time looking up toward a bare twenty-five watt bulb.

William Cheever's name was fourth of four on the frosted glass panel of the door. It wasn't a law firm, it was one of those set-ups where a number of unsuccessful professional men get together to share the rent and the receptionist and the futility.

The receptionist was as light as a Negro can be and still have Negroid features. She had relentlessly straightened her hair and then recurled it in neo-Grecian twists. She wore a high-necked and lace-fringed blouse designed for the bustless girls of midtown, and she was far too ample for it. Looking at her dressed in it, the first word that came to mind was "unsanforized."

She smiled at me and closed a slim volume of Langston Hughes, one finger marking the place. "May I help you?" Her accent was softly British, so she was probably Jamaican.

"William Cheever," I said. I hoped the attorneys at least had separate offices.

"He isn't in this morning."

"Oh." I frowned as worriedly as I could. "I wanted to get in touch with him. As soon as possible. Would you have any idea when he'd be back?"

"Mister Cheever? Oh, no. He very seldom comes to the office." She withdrew the finger from the Langston Hughes book. "In fact, to tell you the honest truth, I sometimes wonder why he has an office here at all."

"Doesn't he meet his clients here?"

"Not so's you'd notice it." She'd been dying to talk about Cheever for days, maybe weeks. "The only clients of Mr. Cheever's that *I've* ever seen," she said archly, "are those gamblers and bookmakers and numbers sellers that he sends here for Mr. Partridge to represent." She leaned confidentially forward, her bosom bracketing Langston Hughes. "Personally, I think Mr. Cheever is *using* Mr. Partridge, giving him business like that. I think it can do terrible harm to Mr. Partridge's reputation as a courtroom lawyer if he becomes linked in the public mind with hoodlums and gamblers."

I smiled at her earnestness and the well-memorized sentence, phrased and rephrased in countless imaginary dialogues. "Once you marry Mr. Partridge," I told her, "you'll be able to overcome Mr. Cheever's influence, I'm sure."

She blushed. She was light enough to do it beautifully. Her fingers fussed with the papers on her desk.

I was sorry to embarrass her, she was a pleasant girl. But she would sooner answer my question if distracted. I said, "Could you give me Mr. Cheever's home address? I do have to talk to him today."

"Yes, of course!" She was overwhelmingly grateful at something else to think about. She scooped up a small notebook and leafed through it. I borrowed pencil and paper and copied down the address. It was only a few blocks away, on 110th Street, a building facing the park on the north side.

It was a sprawling old stone apartment building, dating back to Harlem's days of eminence, when all four sides of the park were limited to the white well-to-do. It had fallen since. Plaster peeled in the huge foyer. The same drab obscenity was scratched seven times in the elevator walls. The eighth floor corridor was marred by bubbled, cracked, dry and eroded paint crumbling from the walls. I went through a gray door marked SERVICE E-H. I was in a small pentagonal gray room. Bags of rubbish leaned against the walls. The concrete floor was a darker gray. The four doors curving around me in Cinemascope each had a letter scrawled on it in white paint, far less professionally than on the front apartment entrances out along the corridor.

The door marked G was locked. I stopped when I realized how relieved that made me.

I had killed one man without meaning to. I had killed

another man in the midst of rapid action, without having a chance to think about it. I had no idea whether I could kill a man coldly and intentionally.

What if I couldn't? To talk of revenge is one thing, but what if I couldn't do it?

I forced into my mind my last picture of Dad, dying in terror, spewing blood. I thought of Bill, and the wife I hadn't met. I remembered how I had looked in the full-length mirror at Lake George. I felt the dead seed in my head where a small glass football could not replace an eye. I looked at the jagged hole that had been clawed into my life.

But it did no good. I didn't hate Cheever. I didn't hate any of them. I felt a sad lonely pity for myself, and that was all.

Wasted, it was all wasted. I was frail and ineffectual, I'd come all this way for nothing.

I leaned back against the entrance door and slid down it till I was sitting on the floor, knees high before my chest, raincoat bunched around my hips. I crossed my forearms on my knees and rested my brow on my arms. Weak, and wasted, and meaningless. Lost, and broken, and impotent.

Until I got mad, at myself. I raised my head and glowered at the white-painted G and whispered stupid insults at myself in idiotic fury. And then after a while that dulled too, and I just sat there, legs stretched out now, and looked at the bags of rubbish, and let my head do whatever it wanted.

I sat there about two hours. When I got up my back was stiff, but I had my role straightened out. I had jerrybuilt a justification for my existence. I was a weak and unworthy vessel, but I would take the life from William Cheever and the other one. If I had been strong and capable, I could kill them out of a cold fury, a dispassionate rage. Instead, I would kill them cheaply, I would kill them only because that was what I was supposed to do.

Back doors get cheap locks. A nail file between door and jamb worked as well as a key in the lock. I pushed the door open silently, and entered the kitchen. Some rooms ahead, I could hear the murmur of talking.

I went left through an empty bedroom. The door was closed, but didn't set snug. Through the crack, I saw him in the living room, talking on the phone. I could only see a narrow strip of the room, so I couldn't tell if he were alone.

He was abusing the receptionist for having given away the secret of his address. His face was naked and jagged and gray. I was glad he was afraid of me.

It hurt him that he couldn't let the girl know just how strongly he was upset. He was having trouble restraining himself, keeping his voice down. He was making do as best he could with heavy sarcasm and cruel caricature of her accent. At last he said, "No, he hasn't come here. How long ago was he there?—It's over two hours. You should have called me, sweetheart, and not wait around till I called you.—Honey, none of my clients are ofay, you know that. When was the last time you saw a white man in that office? Oh, the hell, why waste time talking to you? Besides, it's time for you and Benny Partridge to have lunch together on his sofa, isn't it?—What do you *suppose* I mean, dumplin'?"

He listened a few seconds more, then slammed the receiver down and glared desperately around the room. The way his eyes moved, I could tell he was alone. I reached in under the raincoat and jacket and dragged out Smitty's gun.

Cheever reached for the phone again. He dialed jerkily. I counted ten numbers, so he was calling someone out of town. He told the operator his number, and then he waited, fumbling a Viceroy out of the pack one-handed. All at once he dropped the pack and said quickly into the phone, "Let me talk to Ed. Willy Cheever.—Yeah, sure, I'll hold on."

He managed to get the cigarette out and lit before he had to talk again. Then he said, "Ed? Willy Cheever. Somebody came around to my office this morning, asking for me.—Well, the thing is, the stupid girl at the office gave him my address.—I'm home now. I want to come up, Ed. If I could stay at the farm just a couple days— Just a couple days, Ed, until—Ed, for God's sake, she told him where I live!—There isn't anyplace else.—Ed, I've never asked you for any special favor before. I—Ed! Ed!"

He jiggled the receiver and I stepped into the living room and said, "He hung up on you, Willy."

His head swiveled around and he stared at me. He didn't move. I had Smitty's gun in my right hand. I went over and took the phone out of his hand and cradled it. Then I backed off from him and said, "You better pick up your cigarette. It's burning the rug."

He picked it up, moving like a robot, and put it in the ashtray beside the phone. It smoldered there, and he stared at the gun.

I said, "Ganolese threw you away. He's got too much to worry about, and you're just a cheap Harlem shyster. He can replace you with a nod of his head."

"No." The word jolted out of him. His hands started to twitch together in his lap. "Ed listens to me. Ed respects my advice."

"He threw you away."

"Oh, God!" His hands snapped up and covered his face.

I crossed the room and sat down opposite him and waited for him to finish. When he finally took his hands down, his eyes were red and puffed, his flat cheeks gleamed wet. The little mustache was only silly, like a little girl wearing her mother's shoes. He said, "He called me boy. Like the kid who shines his shoes."

"Eddie Kapp is taking over," I said. "Ganolese doesn't have time for shoe-shine boys. Not even if they went to college."

"He's a son of a bitch. Goddamn him, I treated him right."

"Drive me up there. I'll put in a good word for you with Eddie Kapp."

He stared at me a second, than shook his head. "Not a chance. Not a chance."

"Ganolese is losing. If he was winning, he'd have the time to kid you along like always."

"Oh, *damn!*" His eyes squeezed shut and he pounded the chair arms with clenched fists. "I never tommed!" he cried. "I never sucked! He treated me like a white man, he never made me play the color!"

"That was when he needed you." I got to my feet.

"Take me up there."

He was calming again. He brooded at the wall. "He shouldn't have hung up on me," he whispered. "He shouldn't have called me boy. He's a slick wop, he's nothing but."

"Come along," I said.

He looked at me, and started to calculate. "You'll put in a good word for me with Kapp?"

It was easy to lie to him. "I will," I said. "You've got no reason not to trust me."

"All right," he said. And bought himself an hour or two more of life.

Twenty-Five

His car was this year's Buick, cream and blue, half a block away in a tow-away zone. He had a special permit in the windshield that let him park there.

He drove across 110th westward and turned north and boarded the Henry Hudson Parkway. I sat beside him, Smitty's gun in my lap. We didn't talk.

He took the George Washington Bridge into Jersey, and 17 a while. General Motors cars are all very much alike. The last time I rode this way, it was with Dad in an Oldsmobile one year older than this Buick. I was sitting in the same seat. I felt the nervousness creeping up from my stomach.

He left 17 and crossed the Jersey border back into New York State, still heading north. I said the first words spoken by either of us in the car: "How much farther?"

He looked quick at me, and then out at the highway again. "A little ways beyond Monsey," he said. "Up in Rockland County."

"What's this Monsey? A town?"

"Yes. Small town, built up in the last few years."

"Then they'll have a shopping center. Stop at a sporting goods store."

"All right."

After a while, he turned off the highway on a curving exit that took us under the road we'd just been on and, a little farther, over the Thruway. Then we were on 59, which was lined with newish stores fronted by blacktop parking spaces. Cheever braked nose-in before a sports shop with shotguns and hip boots displayed in the window.

I took the key out of the ignition. I'd already checked the glove compartment and it was clean. I said, "You wait here."

"Don't worry," he said. He had some of his bounce back. "All I can count on now is you and Eddie Kapp. I won't try to run away from you."

"Glad to hear it," I said. The fact that, under other circumstances, I might have liked this smooth and quiet collegian only irritated me.

I bought, in the store, a .30-.30 rifle and a box of cartridges. It cost me a hundred eighty dollars, almost all I had with me.

Back in the car, Cheever drove again while I read the instruction booklet and practiced loading the rifle. Then Cheever said, "About a mile more up this way."

We were passing an intersection. There was undeveloped land around us, and a general store called Willow Tree Corner. I said, "Is the house right out on the road?"

"No. It's set back about half a mile. All uphill from the road. There's a dirt road in."

"Will there—slow down a minute—will there be people watching out at this end of the dirt road?"

"Yeah, there will. That's why I had to get permission to come up. I wouldn't want to turn in there without permission."

"All right. Then go on by. But point it out to me."

"All right."

"You can drive faster again now."

A couple of minutes later he said, "That's it. On the right."

I saw a dirt road that jolted down a bank and curved into the trees. There was a thick wood along here, climbing a steep slope away from the road toward the Ramapo Mountains. I caught just a glimpse of an automobile parked in the road under the trees.

Cheever said, "Now what?"

"Make the first right you can."

About a mile farther on we turned right. It was a smaller road, asphalt, climbing steeply upward. Incongruously, there was suddenly, to our left, a small gravel parking area and a fireplace and picnic table and mesh rubbish basket. I said, "U-turn, and stop over there."

The car was too big and the road too small. He had to back and fill. No other cars came along. It was Monday, the tenth of October, the wrong time of year for traffic on this road.

Cheever stopped on the gravel and pulled on the emergency brake. I got the keys out of the ignition and climbed out of the car. I carried the rifle and Smitty's revolver over and set them on the picnic table.

Cheever came over after me. I said, "Sit down here."

Something in my face or voice tipped him off. He stopped, across the table from me, and looked at my face, warily. His hands were out in front of him, the fingers splayed wide apart. He said, "What is it? What's the matter?"

I said, "Do you know who I am?"

"You were with Kapp. Up at Lake George. You were the one came up to the car."

"But do you know my name?"

He shook his head.

I said, "Ray Kelly. Will Kelly's son."

He kept shaking his head. "It doesn't mean a thing to me. I don't know what you think, but you're wrong."

"Kill the Kellys," I said. "That's what I'm thinking. Somebody whispered that in Ed Ganolese's ear. Kill the Kellys, kill them all. The old man and both sons and the daughter-in-law. The whole tribe, because Eddie Kapp is coming out of Dannemora, and we can't be sure—"

He cried, "No! You got it all wrong! It wasn't me!"

"Because we can't be sure," I finished, "which boy is Eddie Kapp's son, and even if we get the right one, some other member of the family might stand in for him, and Ed you know how sentimental those old wops can get. Isn't that right, Cheever? Somebody whispered that to Ed Ganolese, and then he pointed the finger."

His head was shaking again, and he was backing away

from me, away from the table. "Not me!" he was crying. "You got it all wrong, Kelly, you got to believe me! It wasn't like that, it wasn't *like* that!"

"You set the whole thing in motion, Cheever," I said. I picked up Smitty's gun.

He turned and went running off into the woods, away from the road. In just a second, he was out of sight, and I could hear the sounds of his thrashing getting farther away.

I should have killed him. I could have. When he took his first running step, I had the revolver on him. There was one fraction of a second there when I was sighting down the top of the revolver barrel right into his left side, under his arm, his arm up in the running motion, and my brain told my finger to squeeze the trigger. And it didn't.

I lowered my arm, and listened to him tumbling away through the woods, ripping his trouser legs, catching his shoelaces in the tough weeds, falling and scrabbling and running scared.

I couldn't kill him. I told myself it was because I wasn't sure of him, because there was still a chance it was somebody else who'd done the whispering in Ganolese's ear. There were other reasons why he might have been the one picked to go up to Lake George.

It was true. But it wasn't the reason. I hadn't killed him because I couldn't kill him.

He was gone. The woods were silent. Right doesn't make might.

I went over and tossed the keys on the front seat of the car. I picked up the rifle and the revolver, and went across the road and into the woods on the other side, heading toward where the farm hideout should be.

I had to kill Ed Ganolese. I *had* to.

Twenty-Six

It was late afternoon, the sun was orange-red low in the sky behind me. It was evening dark there under the trees. I kept my direction by following the slant of the long red sunbeams.

I came to the dirt road first. I stepped out on it before I knew it was there, and then I pulled back into the trees again. I stood still and listened. Off to my right I could hear faint sounds of men talking. That would be the guards, down near the road. I turned left and moved slowly uphill through the trees, keeping close to the road.

The farmhouse was painted yellow. It was two stories high and sprawling. Three cars were parked in front of it, a black Cadillac and a tan-and-cream Chrysler and a green Buick. Four men sat on the stoop, talking together in monotones.

The house was shabby. Stretching away to the right, along a leveling of the ground, was what had once been cleared land. Behind and to the right of the main house was the barn.

Keeping to the woods, I circled to the left around the house. Once past it, the ground sloped more sharply uphill. I climbed until I could come around directly behind the house, and then I moved slowly back down to the nearest safe point. Then I sat down with my back to a tree, and watched the rear windows, and waited.

It got dark almost as suddenly as turning off a light. Then it got colder. The jacket and raincoat weren't enough to keep the cold out. I stood and walked back and forth, flapping my arms.

From time to time, a light went on in one of the back rooms. Whenever that happened I stopped my prowling around to study the room and the people in it. I saw the kitchen, and a number of bedrooms. There were a lot of people in the house, men and women both. But it was almost ten o'clock before I finally saw Ed Ganolese.

He came into the kitchen and got a glass from the cupboard and ice cubes from the refrigerator. There were bottles on the drainboard. He stood with his back to me and made himself a drink.

I'd been out there nearly five hours. My hands were cold and I hadn't chanced smoking a cigarette. Now I was afraid my aim wouldn't be any good. I'd always done well with the carbine in the Air Force, but this was a different weapon and I was shivering and I was nervous for need of a cigarette.

So I let him go the first time. I hunched over with my back to the house and lit a cigarette, and stood behind a tree smoking it, my hands under my jacket pressed against my sides. When the cigarette was gone, I checked through the scope again. The kitchen was empty.

This wasn't any good. I hadn't been able to kill Cheever. Now I'd seen Ganolese in the sights, the chiefest devil, and I'd found another reason not to pull the trigger.

I couldn't let that weakness come over me again, the way

it had with Cheever. I had to do this, and get it over with.

The sky was overcast, with no moon. I moved down the slope closer to the house, until I was nearly down to the level of the kitchen windows. I was in the open now, but I couldn't be seen from the house. I was beyond the rectangles of light from the windows.

I crouched, the rifle leaning against my shoulder, my hands kept warm against my sides beneath my jacket. And when Ganolese came back to the kitchen, the empty glass in his hand, I refused to think of excuses.

I was so close now that his white-shirted back filled the scope. I got into kneeling position, as I'd been taught in the service. Right knee on the ground, left knee up, left elbow over left knee. I sighted down to his left shoulder blade in the white expanse of his shirt, and when I fired, the barrel kicked up and for a second I couldn't find the kitchen window through the sight. I didn't hear the sound of the shot at all.

When I found the window again, Ganolese was slowly folding forward over the drainboard, bottles skittering away down the slope into the sink. A tiny dot of darkish red had stained the back of his shirt, low and to the right of where I'd aimed.

I fired again, a bit high and to the left, and this time I was ready for the recoil, and I kept the target in the sight, and saw the bullet kick him forward, and the second red dot form, and then he slid down out of sight and I got to my feet, the rifle slack in my right hand.

Then sound came back to the world. I hadn't heard either shot, or anything else between them, but now all at once, as though a radio volume knob had been turned up,

I heard men calling and shouting to one another, and even the sound of heavy feet running on wooden floors inside the house.

I turned and went back up into the woods and over to the right, moving slowly in the blackness. I kept moving for half an hour or more, only the slope of the land keeping me going in a straight line. When I stopped, I was alone in silence. There was no pursuit.

I sank down against a tree to wait for dawn. It got deadly cold. I slept fitfully, dreaming of ogres and childish things. Every time I awoke again, I smoked a bitter cigarette, cupping my hands around it for warmth.

With dawn, I stood and moved around, trying to get warmth back into my body. But I kept near the same tree until the sun was up. Then I walked back through the damp woods to the house, leaving Smitty's gun and the rifle against the tree.

It was deserted. All the cars were gone. I walked down the dirt road to the asphalt two-laner and turned left. A woman in a station wagon with two young kids and a Doberman pinscher gave me a lift to Suffern. I got a bus there for New York. I went back to the hotel room and took a long hot shower and went to bed. I slept fourteen hours, without dreams, and woke up drugged, to find there was mail for me.

It was a letter from Uncle Henry, a thick envelope fat with papers. There was a note from him, telling me to be careful, telling me I should come home to Binghamton. There were documents to be signed, about Bill's house and Bill's car and Bill's kid. And there was a clipping from the *Binghamton Press*.

In the note, Uncle Henry said about the clipping, "This ought to relieve your mind." The clipping showed a photograph of a scared balding man in a dark suit, his elbow held by a sun-glassed policeman. The story with the photograph told how methodical police laboratory work had finally cracked the hit-run accident of August 29th, in which Mrs. Ann Kelly, mother of one, had been killed. The driver of the death car was an electrical appliance salesman from Scranton, named Drugay.

He had nothing to do with the Organization at all.

Twenty-Seven

Eddie Kapp lied to me. He lied to me.

The Organization didn't kill my sister-in-law.

He lied to me. In some ways, in every way, in how many ways I didn't know.

Why did he lie to me? So I would stay with him.

But if he wanted me to stay with him, then his lies should have been the truth. His lies made sense, or there was no sense in his wanting me to stay with him.

He said I was a symbol, around which his cronies would gather. Was that a lie? If so, it had no purpose. His cronies *had* gathered around him. Nick Rovito had tested me. No one had asked what I was doing there. So how could that have been a lie?

He said Ed Ganolese knew about the symbol, and was trying to destroy it. Was that a lie? But a tan-and-cream Chrysler had killed my father, and had tried to kill me.

And the same tan-and-cream Chrysler had tried to kill Eddie Kapp. And the same tan-and-cream Chrysler had been parked at the farm where Ed Ganolese was hiding out. So how could that have been a lie?

Or was it only half a lie?

I was alive. *I* was alive.

The tan-and-cream Chrysler had pulled up beside us, thirty-eight miles from New York, and the man on the right-hand side had reached out his arm and shot my father. That was all.

They must have known my father was dead. They must have seen their bullets hit. And they had driven on.

They hadn't stopped to be sure that *I* was dead. They hadn't even fired a shot at me.

They hadn't been *trying* to kill me. They had killed the man Ed Ganolese had pointed at. Will Kelly.

He was the symbol. The trusted lawyer, the right-hand man from the old days. The others might have objected that Eddie Kapp was too old, that he couldn't handle the whole operation by himself, or that he might die very soon after they'd made their coup, and then there'd only be another power fight, and they wouldn't want two fights like that so close together. So there was a second man, a younger man, the trusted lawyer, who knew the operation and who could handle its administration, a man they could all agree on to succeed Eddie Kapp. Will Kelly.

Without Will Kelly, Kapp couldn't rally the others around him. So Ganolese had Kelly murdered.

And Eddie Kapp had given up. He'd written his sister, he'd planned his retirement. And then I came along.

He hadn't been sure it would work. He'd had to talk and

argue and reason and explain for a week on the telephone at Lake George, before the others would go along with it.

I could almost hear the way he'd put it: "Here's my son, Ray Kelly. Will Kelly took care of him for me while I was out of circulation. Will trained him, gave him the background, explained the set-up to him. The boy's young, but he knows what's going on, and he learns fast. He'll take over when I'm gone, and he won't be greedy, he'll be content with New York. And there'll be forty, fifty years in him."

It took him a week, and probably a lot more arguments than that, but he talked them into it. And he gave me that song-and-dance about me as a symbol because he knew I didn't want to have anything to do with his mob. Once he was in the driver's seat, after the coup, he didn't care how many of his cronies knew the truth.

I'd told him about Bill's wife being killed. That gave him the idea to sell me that family-purge story. Because then all he had to do was point me. I was a loaded gun, held by Eddie Kapp.

Bill. My brother Bill.

When I'd left Lake George, I thought I was ridding myself of Eddie Kapp forever. I wasn't. I had to find him again. Now.

Twenty-Eight

That afternoon, I went up to Riverdale. It was just a week to the day since the revolution had started. Five days ago, the first sign of the counterattack had appeared in the papers, when Patros Kanzantkos fell down the stairs in his Riverdale home and broke his neck. The address was given in the newspaper story.

I took the subway as far as it would go, looking out at the big-shouldered, dull brick apartment buildings when the train became an elevated in the Bronx. At the last stop, I got a cab. I had three hundred more in my pocket from Bill's dwindling bank account. Bill's Luger was huge and bulky against my side, tucked under my belt. The raincoat was supposed to cover it.

The house was colonial-style, two stories, white, in a very good section, all curving roads and trees and backyard wading pools. There was a black wreath still on the door.

The obituary notice had said that Kanzantkos was survived by a wife, Emilie, and a son, Robert. It was the son who answered the doorbell, an angry black-haired boy of my chronological age, his face marred by a petulant mouth, his black suit oddly awkward on his frame.

I said, "I'd like to talk to your mother, please."

He said, insolently, "What about?"

"Tell her Eddie Kapp's son is here."

"Why should she care?"

"If she wants you to know, she'll tell you."

That struck a nerve. He paled, and when he said, "Wait there," his voice was harsher, more strained.

He closed the door, and I lit a cigarette and looked at the careful rock garden fronting the pretty house across the way. And then he came back and said, "All right. Come on in." He was still angry.

I followed him upstairs to a small room furnished with two sofas and a stereophonic record player. The walls were ranked with bookcases holding record albums. Mrs. Kanzantkos, a small and brittle woman with a narrow nose, said, "Thank you, Bobby. I'll want to talk to Mr. Kapp alone."

He went away, glowering, reluctantly closing the door. I said, "He doesn't know what his father did for a living?"

She said, "No. And he never will."

"A boy should always know who and what his father is," I said.

Coldly, she said, "I'll be the judge of that, Mr. Kapp."

"Kelly," I corrected her. "Ray Kelly."

Instantly she was on her feet. "You said you were Eddie Kapp's son."

"I am. I was brought up by a man named Kelly."

The distrust didn't all leave her eyes. "And what do you want from me?"

"I was with my father when he got out of Dannemora," I said, "and at the meeting at Lake George. I met your husband there. He mentioned me, didn't he?"

"Mr. Kanzantkos rarely discussed business with me," she said.

"All right. The point is, my father and I were separated after Lake George. I had another job to do. Now it's done, and I want to get in touch with him again."

"I would have no idea where you could find him."

"I know that. But you must know at least one or two of the other people who were at Lake George. I wish you'd call one of them and tell him I'm here."

"Why?"

"I want to get together with my father again. Isn't that natural?"

"And he didn't tell you where you could get in touch with him?"

"We parted hastily. I had this other thing to do."

"What other thing?"

"I had to kill a man named Ed Ganolese."

She blinked. The silence was like wool. Then she got to her feet. "Wait here," she said. "I—I'll call someone."

"Thank you."

She seemed glad to leave the room. She closed the door softly after her.

Ten minutes later, the door opened again, and the son came slipping in. He shut the door after him and leaned against it and said, his voice low, "I want to know what's going on."

"Nothing's going on," I said.

"She's keeping something from me," he insisted. "You know what it is. You tell me."

I shook my head.

"Why are you here?"

"It has nothing to do with you."

"My father?"

"No."

"That's a lie. Who's my mother calling?"

"I have no idea."

He came away from the door, arms high. "I'll twist it out of you—"

Before I had to do anything to him, the door opened and his mother was standing there. She ordered him from the room, and he refused to go until he found out what all the mystery was. They screamed at each other for five minutes or more. I spent the time looking at the record collection. Classical music and stringed dinner music. One small section of Dixieland jazz.

When at last Robert left, his mother said to me, "I'm sorry. He should have known better."

"As you say, it's your business."

"Yes. I phoned a friend of my husband's. He promised to call back as soon as possible. Would you like to come down to the kitchen for coffee?"

"Thank you."

The kitchen was white and chintz. Through the window, I could see a well tended back lawn and a flagstone patio. Rose bushes lined the fence at the back of the property. From the cellar came the drumming rhythm of someone at a punching bag. That would be Robert, forcing me to talk.

We waited in silence. She didn't ask me any questions. We sat there twenty minutes before the phone rang in another room on the ground floor. She excused herself and went away, coming back a minute later to say, "He wants to talk to you."

It was Kapp. He said, "Ray? Is that you?"

"Yes, Kapp, it's me."

"You recognized my voice?"

"Why not?"

"That was you got Ganolese Monday night?"

"That was me."

"I'll be a son of a bitch." He sounded happy, and half-drunk. "You lovely little bastard, you're a chip off the old block. You're done now, huh?"

"I'm done. It's squared away. And there's nothing else for me to do. I'd like to stick with you."

"Goddamn it, Ray, you don't know how that makes me feel. Oh, goddamn it, boy, that's great. I hoped to God you'd decide that."

"I'm glad," I said. "I came looking for you right away, as soon as I was done with the other."

"Do you want me to send a car?"

"Are you in the city? If you are, it'd be quicker for me to take the subway."

"Sure thing. We've got ourselves a suite at the Weatherton. That's at Lexington and 52nd."

"I know where it is."

"It's under the name Peterson. Raymond Peterson. You remember?"

"I remember. I'll be right there."

I hung up, and the woman said, "I'll drive you to the subway, if you want."

"Thank you."

We went out to the garage. From the cellar came the drumming of the punching bag.

Twenty-Nine

I walked the block from the subway stop to the Weatherton Hotel. I remembered it. It was the one where Dad had stayed, where we'd both stayed the night before they killed him. Kapp wouldn't know that.

I asked for Mr. Peterson's suite, and they sent my name up, then told me the fifteenth floor. I rode up in the elevator. 1512 was to the left. I could hear party sounds.

I knocked on the door and a smiling man with a broken nose opened it and said, "You're Kapp's kid, huh?"

"That's right."

"Put her there! He keeps tellin' us how great you are!"

His hand was huge, but soft. I shook it, and went inside.

The suite went on and on, room after room. A nervous little man took over from the first one and showed me my bedroom. I left the Luger on the bed, under the raincoat. Then I followed the nervous man through more rooms to the party.

It was a huge parlor, with French doors leading to the terrace. A radio played bad music in one corner, competing with a television set across the way. Sectional sofas and coffee tables were scattered all around. Two portable bars stood full and handy.

There were about thirty people in the room, maybe ten of them women. The women all had high breasts and professional smiles. The men were laughing and shouting at one another.

Kapp had one of the women in a corner. He was talking steadily to her, and his right hand kneaded her breast. She kept smiling.

Somebody saw me and shouted, "Hey, Kapp! Here's your kid!"

He looked around and then came running over. Behind him, the woman smoothed out the wrinkles with a little contemptuous shrug, but kept smiling.

Kapp punched my arm and hugged me and shouted at me how great I was. Then he pranced me all around the room, introducing me to all the men and telling them all how great I was. He didn't introduce me to any of the women, but they all kept watching me.

For fifteen minutes, it all whirled around. Half a dozen people told me the reason for the celebration. The national committee had given the nod. They were in. Coup successful. And they all had me to thank, because bumping Ganolese had done the trick. That was what had clinched it. There was only a little reorganizing left to do, and from there on life was gravy.

Kapp finally calmed down a bit, and people stopped shouting in my ear. I took his arm and said, "Kapp, I want to talk to you. I want to tell you about it."

"Goddamn it, boy," he said, grinning at me. "Let's get away from this mob."

I led the way toward the bedroom where I'd left the raincoat. On the way we came across the nervous man, hurrying somewhere. I grabbed his elbow and said, "Come along with us for a minute."

Kapp said, "What the hell for?"

I said, "You'll see."

We all went into the bedroom and Kapp said, "What the hell do you want Mouse here for?"

"He's my messenger," I said. I reached under the raincoat and took out the Luger and held it on them as I closed and locked the bedroom door.

Kapp stared at the gun, and sobriety washed down his face like lye. He said, "What the hell are you up to?"

I said, "Mouse, you listen close. My name is Ray Kelly. Eddie Kapp is my natural father, my father by blood. Isn't that right, Kapp?"

"Sure that's right. Why the hell—?"

"Hold on. You got that part, Mouse?"

He nodded jerkily, his eyes on the gun.

"All right. I also had a mother and a foster father and a half-brother and a sister-in-law. My mother killed herself because of Eddie Kapp here. Isn't that right, Kapp?"

Relief hit him so hard he sat down heavily on the edge of the bed. "Oh, for God's sake, Ray, that was twenty-one years ago. And who knew she was going to do something like that? You pull a gun on me for something twenty-one years old?"

"I'll get more current in a minute. Just hold on. About my mother, and Will Kelly. He was your sideman, he worked with you every step of the way. You were just about to make the move, take control of the New York organization, and Will Kelly was an active part of it, working right next to you all the way. Then somebody sicked the Federal Government on you because—"

"Ganolese," he said. "That filthy bastard, Ganolese."

"—because of your taxes. The government put you out of the way, so Ganolese could take over instead of you. And Will Kelly had to get out of town. His wife couldn't stand the small town life, but she didn't dare come back to New York. She killed herself."

"Twenty-one years ago, Ray. For God's sake—"

"Shut up. I told you I'd get more current. You knew you were getting out September 15th. You got word to Will Kelly, one way or another, that you were going to make the move again. And you started lining people up, telling them Kelly was going to be with you. The word got to Ganolese. He had Kelly killed."

"You're a sharp boy, Ray," he said. "You figured that

out all by yourself." He wasn't really worried at all yet.

"I figured more than that," I told him. "Those people out there at the party wouldn't buy you without Will Kelly. Without somebody reasonably young as the heir-apparent. They figured you were too old."

"Not Eddie Kapp. I'll live to a hundred."

"No, you won't. I'm not done yet. My sister-in-law got killed in a hit-run accident. They caught the guy."

"Good for them," he said.

"Up till I showed up, you thought you were through. You wrote your sister, you figured to retire. Then you saw me, and it was worth a try, see if you could get the boys to accept me rather than my father."

"*I'm* your father, Ray."

"You sired me. It isn't the same thing. You knew I wasn't interested in your empire, so you gave me that song and dance about family and symbols, to talk me into sticking with you. When I told you my sister-in-law had been killed, that gave you the idea. If she hadn't died, you wouldn't have been able to pull it."

"I would of thought of something else." He grinned like a banker. "Aren't you proud of your old man, boy? I think on my feet."

"Not for much longer. There's one more. My brother Bill. He was killed, too. He was my half-brother by blood, just as you're my father by blood. And you've always got to avenge blood." I turned to Mouse. "You've always got to avenge blood, Mouse? Isn't that right?"

He swallowed noisily, and bobbed his head.

"Now, Mouse, Eddie Kapp here killed my brother Bill."

Kapp jumped up from the bed, howling. "What the goddamn hell are you talking about? For Christ's sake, why would I do a stupid thing like that?"

"You wanted me with you, or you wouldn't be leading the revolt. You were afraid, once I found out Will Kelly wasn't my father, I'd stop, I'd lose heart and give the thing up. Same as if I found out he was still part of the mob, all this time. And then I wouldn't stick with you for a second. So you murdered Bill. I was supposed to think Ganolese did that one, too, and you could offer the partnership. 'We both want the same people, only for different reasons.' That's exactly what you said."

He shook his head. "You got it wrong, Ray. I was with you from the time Bill went upstairs to the time we found him dead."

"No. You were gone ten minutes, to the head. And nobody else could have gotten their hands on Bill's gun. He would have put it on the dresser. Any stranger came in, the gun would have been in Bill's hand. You could go in and talk to him, tell him you want to be friends, and walk around the room until you angle over to the dresser, and there you are."

When he moved, it was dirty. He jumped for Mouse, trying to shove him into me. I ran back and to the side, jumping up onto the bed and down on the floor on the other side, turning to face the door. He had his hand on the key when I shot him. I emptied the Luger into him before he could hit the floor.

Mouse lay quivering on his stomach on the floor, arms over his head in stupid protectiveness. I wiped my prints from the Luger and dropped it on the floor and went around to poke Mouse in the side with my toe. I said, "Get up. I'm not finished talking to you."

It took him a while to get his limbs working right. I waited till he was standing, then I said, "You wait till I leave here. You give me a good five minutes. Then you go back to the party and tell them what happened. And tell them why it happened. You got that?"

He nodded. There was white all around the pupils of his eyes.

"This was a blood matter," I told him, "not a mob matter. Blood revenging blood. There's no need for them to come after me, to avenge Eddie Kapp. I'm his son, and I say there's no need for it. And I don't remember a single name or a single face that I saw here today or at Lake George two weeks ago. You got that?"

He nodded again.

"Five minutes," I said.

I went out to the hall. The party was raging to my left, too loud for them to have heard the shots in that closed and bulkily furnished bedroom. I walked down to the right. The big man with the broken nose was sitting in a fragile chair by the door. He said, "What they doing? Shooting guns off the terrace? They'll get cops up here if they don't look out."

"I hope it's over pretty soon," I said. "I need my sleep."

"You moving in?"

"Just going to get my luggage."

"You won't get much sleep here." He laughed. "This'll go on for a couple days yet."

I left, and took the elevator down, and went out to the street.

Thirty

I went into the first bar I came to on Lexington Avenue, but it was lunchtime and full of bland smooth people. I stayed only long enough for one shot of bar whiskey on the rocks and one long session emptying my stomach into the toilet in the men's room. Then I headed west.

It was all bland and arid till Sixth Avenue. My stomach was empty, but from time to time I had to lean against light standards and wait through an attack of dry heaves. On Sixth Avenue I found a White Rose, where the drinks were ample and cheap.

I couldn't stay in one place. I spent about an hour in that first place, and then moved downtown, stopping for a while in each bar I came to. At four in the morning, another guy and I were thrown out of a place somewhere downtown, and the other guy said he knew a great place to sleep out of the wind, behind a theater. We went there, and someone was sleeping there, with a half-full bottle of wine. We took it away from him and found another place, and went to sleep. But before we did, I tried to tell him all my troubles. I couldn't enunciate very well, and he couldn't concentrate at all, so he never found out that I was trying to tell him that I had killed my father.

In the morning, I woke up first, freezing cold and with a bitter grinding headache. I finished the wine and felt better, somewhat warmer, and the headache fuzzier.

From there, it all blended in together. I got in a

couple of fights, and once I went to a place in New
Jersey late at night where the bars opened at five. I
threw up in the H & M tubes.

Until one morning I woke up in a great gray metal box.
The sides of the box were all incredibly far away. The top
of the box kept coming closer and then receding. Other
human beings were in the metal box with me, making
small and ghastly noises.

I don't know how long I lay on the floor before I realized I was in a room and not a box, nor how much longer
before I realized I was in a jail. In the drunk tank.

First time crept, and then it leaped up and flew a
while on wide black wings. I tried to count to sixty, to get
in my mind how long a minute should be, but when I
started to count my brain scraped against the inside of
my skull and I cried out because I thought I was going to
die. A lot of people grumbled and shouted at me to be
quiet. I rolled over on my stomach and pressed my forehead against the cold floor and waited.

It did finally lessen, and I could sit up. And then I
could stand, and take stock of myself.

My shoes were gone. So was my wallet. So were my
raincoat and my suitcoat and my tie. So were my watch
and belt and high school ring. So was my glass eye.

I found an empty bit of wall to sit and lean against, and
dozed and wept and by the time a jailer came and opened
the clanging door and called my name, the worst was
over. I was empty, in every way.

I followed him to a small narrow room with a wooden
table and four wooden chairs. Johnson stood up from one
of the chairs, and the jailer went away.

We looked at each other. Johnson said, "You get it all out of your system?"

"Yes."

"I've been looking for you. I thought you might wind up here. I've had a friend of mine here keeping an eye out for you."

"What day is it?"

"Tuesday."

"What date?"

"The twenty-fifth. Of October."

One day less than two weeks. "It took me a while, didn't it?"

"I guess you had a lot to get over."

"I guess I did."

"You feel strong enough to go for a walk?"

"Where to?"

"My place first. Get you cleaned up."

"They stole my eye, Johnson."

"We'll get you another one."

He shepherded me like a strayed child. He lived in a ratty apartment on West 46th Street, west of 9th Avenue. I told him the hotel and the name where he could find my suitcase. While he was gone, I showered and shaved. Looking at myself in the mirror, when I started to shave, I got a shock. My face was gaunt and filthy, hair and beard shaggy, the empty eye socket a grim dull red.

When Johnson came back, I was wearing his robe. He brought me an eye patch, till I could get another eye. I dressed out of the suitcase, and then he came over with a bottle of Gordon's gin, only two or three shots gone from it. "Do you want some?"

I shook my head. "Not now. Try me in a couple of weeks. I'll be ready for social drinking then."

"It's all over, then."

"Yes, it really is."

"All right. I've got something for you." He returned the gin bottle to his dresser drawer, under the shirts, and came back with a small envelope. "Two hard types came to the office Friday before last. They said this was for you. If I ran across you anywhere, I should give it to you. I got the feeling I should make an effort to run across you."

I took the envelope and ripped it open. Inside, there were five one hundred dollar bills. And a note: "No hard feelings, L.G."

Johnson watched my face. "Well?"

"I don't get it." I showed it to him.

"You don't know anybody named L.G.?"

Then I got it. Lake George. "I know now," I said. "Never mind."

"They're telling you they won't bother you, is that it?"

"Let's flush that note down the toilet or something."

"Shall I burn it, like Secret Agent X 7?"

"I think you ought to."

He did. Watching it burn in the ashtray, he said, "Do you remember your talk with Winkler?"

"Who?"

"Detective Winkler, of New York's finest."

"I talked to him?"

"You wanted to confess to half the killings in the United States. A couple of racketeers named Ganolese and Kapp, and some old lawyer out on Long Island, and I don't know who all."

"I did?"

"Winkler says it was a real wild story, except you refused to give any names except of the people you killed."

I looked around the room. "Then why am I here? Why didn't he lock me up?"

"Officially, Ganolese and Kapp aren't even missing. No bodies, no murder weapons, no witnesses. Officially, the lawyer died of a heart attack. It said so on the certificate. Winkler says I should tell you not to come bothering him with any more wild stories." He grinned at me.

"They don't care."

"Not about people like Kapp and Ganolese. Not even a little bit."

I stood up and walked around the room and stretched. This was the other side. I came through, and this was the other side.

Johnson emptied the ashtray. "One thing more," he said. "I was looking for you anyway, even before those hard types showed up. Two days after you called me the last time a guy hired me to find you. Arnold Beeworthy, his name is. You mentioned me to him. He said you were supposed to call him back about six weeks ago."

"I forgot about him."

"Tomorrow, why don't you take a run out there and say hello?"

"Okay."

I slept on his sofa. In the morning, I spent two hours being fitted for a new eye. I paid for that out of the five hundred, and gave the rest to Johnson. He didn't want to take it, but I told him he was being paid by the guys who beat him up.

In the afternoon, I took the subway out to Queens. Beeworthy grabbed me the minute he saw me and stuck me in front of the tape recorder. We stopped for dinner and went back at it and didn't quit till midnight. I slept in the guest room. The next morning, he drove me into Manhattan to get my suitcase from Johnson. When we got back, Sara was listening to the tape and crying. Arnie told her to cut that out and make us some coffee.

THE END